CONFESSIONS OF A BACKUP DANCER

CONFESSIONS OF A BACKUP DANCER

BY ANONYMOUS

as told to Tucker Shaw

SIMON PULSE
New York   London   Toronto   Sydney

First Simon & Schuster edition June 2004

Copyright © 2004 by 17th Street Productions, an Alloy company.

Cover copyright © 2004 by 17th Street Productions, an Alloy company.

SIMON & SCHUSTER
An imprint of Simon & Schuster Children's Publishing Division
1230 Avenue of the Americas, New York, NY 10020

Produced by 17th Street Productions,
an Alloy company
151 West 26th Street
New York, NY 10001

Simon Pulse and colophon are registered trademarks of Simon & Schuster, Inc.

Printed in the United States of America
10 9 8 7 6 5 4 3 2 1

Library of Congress Control Number 2003115035
ISBN 0-689-87075-2

Name: Kelly Kimball

Birthday: April 19, 1986. Aries. I just hit the big 1-7 last month. I got a sarong from my boss at Beatz Beachside Dance Studio (see below), two gift certificates to CD Mania from mom and Evan, and this personal diary software from tito.

Address: San Diego, California. That should do it.

Hobbies: dancing. It's pretty much all I do. ever since I was a little kid. First it was tap and ballet. Then jazz. Then modern. Now hip-hop and believe it or not more tap. I kind of like it. It's also my job. Well, sort of. I'm not really a dancer but I work at Beatz Beachside Dance Studio over on san pedro street, which is nowhere near the beachside but whatever. They pay me pretty well (and I SERIOUSLY need the money, especially now that my mom's latest husband pretty much spent all of our savings on his own annoying little perfect-blond twin girls, staci and traci) plus I get to take free classes, which I'd never be able to afford.

Heroes: The girl in Alias. Wade Robson (yeah, he's annoying on that show and everything but he's pretty amazing as a dancer and whatever. that means something to me). Rochelle Ballard, Savion Glover. Britney Spears. (Don't ask, I just like her. I know she doesn't sing as good as Christina or whatever but I don't care I still like her better.) And of course, mostly, Darcy Barnes. Not because I love love love her music or anything, but

1

she's pretty amazing if you ask me and I dig the way she dances. In fact I know pretty much all the routines from her videos. she's definitely the biggest pop star out there. Plus she was pretty funny when she hosted SNL the other night, gotta love that.

Favorite Daydream: Me. Jesse Nixon (that VJ guy or whatever with the spiky little faux mohawk. Or is it faux hawk? Anyway . . .), a deserted beach, big sunset, coconuts, skinny dipping. Maybe a blender. Anyway, add it up. Actually Justin Timberlake would do, too. Or maybe Nick Lachey. Nah, not Nick Lachey. But definitely Justin. And Jesse obviously. Except I heard he was going out with Darcy. Whatever, this is only a daydream so who cares.

Greatest Accomplishment: winning the All-City Modern Dance Invitational and the All-City Hip-Hop Dance Invitational in the same year, last year. I gotta defend my titles this fall.

Most Embarrassing Moment: too many to mention. can I come back to this one?

Favorite Book: Biography of Martha Graham. also I like stephen king books. and I got off on some of those Gossip Girl books too.

Three Reasons to Love Me:

1. I'm always totally honest.

2. I have pretty good taste in clothes, music, and people.

3. I have memorized every dance routine from every

TRL top-3 video not to mention every video on 106 and Park and I have the videotapes to prove it.

note: the diary software made me fill out that dumb form.

I guess they put in that last entry to help boost self-esteem. Frankly, I need all the help I can get in that area. What 17-year-old girl couldn't? I mean, everyone keeps telling us we have none, you know? how all us teen girls are a bunch of insecure, impatient, overindulgent freaks. if a girl's not careful she could start to believe it.

BEATZ BEACHSIDE DANCE STUDIO

SAN DIEGO, 4:45 PM

Outfit: postman pants, black sleeveless tee with small but horrifying deodorant stain under left breast. (Was it there all day?)
Hair: a disaster. the roots aren't funny anymore.
Mood: distracted.
Fortune: Signs can lie. (I'm getting fortunes from this website tito told me about. they send a newsletter to my email every day along with like 35 ads but whatever, I like the fortunes.)

I was seriously bored at work today. Manning the front desk of Beatz Beachside Dance Studio in San Diego can be totally mind-numbing, especially when the only class going on is a seniors swing class in the far studio, studio C. Old people seniors, not high school seniors.

Anyway, I was reading some gossip online about Darcy Barnes and Jesse Nixon, the reigning teen king and queen of the pop universe (as seen on (M)TV!), and how they're supposedly secretly dating or something. the article said something about a house they'd bought together in the Hollywood Hills or one of those places. seems weird that they're dating even though they've known each other since they were like seven and on that Please Don't Do That on Television show or what-ever it was called. I don't know if they're going out or not, but I guess it's kind of fun to think about. and I know one thing, if she's not dating him, she's a fool cause he is FINE.

I was so bored I read the article three times and was starting in on a fourth when the lovely Tito, my best friend in the universe who works at We Bop! the super-expensive tween boutique next door, threw open the front door and rescued me.

"hey girl!" he yelled. "look what I found in the back of the boutique! go try this on." he held out a baby tee with a cowboys and Indians scene on the front.

I go, "Tito I'm gonna look like a waitress at some goofy western-themed bar where the waitresses wear daisy dukes." Tito just goes, "Go try it on. it costs $85."

I was like, "what idiot spends $85 on a baby tee?" then I asked tito to watch the desk for a sec so I could go try it on. I ducked into this empty practice room, slipped off my sleeveless shirt, and pulled the new t-shirt over my head. with mirrors on three sides, I could see immediately that it fit perfectly.

perfectly, that is, if I was, for example, Darcy Barnes.

I mean, this t-shirt *fit*. Tight. My boobs never looked bigger. they weren't darcy barnes's size, of course, because all I got is a b-cup. ok, b-minus. ok, fine, I'm an a.

I stared at my reflection for a while, humming that old-school Darcy Barnes song "Love You Like a Lollipop," which happened to be drifting in from the lobby. swaying, watching my belly button swoop and drop and twist. it was riveting.

it took a moment before I realized I'd actually started doing the steps to "Lollipop," which I'd learned from watching the video about 400 million times. (I have the DVD, so sue me.) Anyway, before I knew it, I was totally going for it. my feet were racing, my head swinging, my hips shaking. the beat was constant but irregular . . . each verse had a bar where the tempo dropped, but I knew when those passages were coming and was ready for them. my body was cruising from beat to beat. I was becoming darcy herself.

I'd done it—I'd entered that zone you reach when you're dancing and you're completely consumed by the music, and your feet bypass your brain and carry your body weightlessly. That place where you stop thinking and start feeling. it doesn't happen every day, in fact it's pretty rare. I guess every dancer probably calls it something different. But Tito and I call it going THERE.

I was two bars away from the part in the video where the guy lifts darcy by one foot and tosses her into a backflip, and I realized I needed a guy. without warning, tito slipped in behind me. I never thought, "Where did he come from?" because Tito's just like that . . . always there when you need him. And THERE when I needed him. His hands came out, my foot went up, and I executed a flawless backflip.

6

Then, just like in the video, Tito faded into the background and I took the last few bars of the song solo. I spun, ground, whirled, and writhed, tito squealing the whole time. "WORK! WORK!"

I guess that means he liked it.

the music changed to some totally stupid Jewel song or something and tito and I went back into the lobby.

he goes, "that was flawless, Kel . . . seriously flawless. you are way better than any of those hooches in the darcy video."

tito is my total positive-feedback support-system best friend, and there's nothing I wouldn't do for him. but this fact sometimes makes me distrust comments like that. like, he's supposed to say that. he's my best friend, you know?

I go, "shut up! besides you could easily be one of the boys in the video. especially the one in the hockey jersey."

he goes shut up. he handed me a Twizzler and goes, "Listen Kelly I know I've got a lot to offer, but you're, like, on another level with the dancing. you're really GOOD. when you dance it feels so REAL. everyone's always talking about REALNESS all the time but you've got it." he goes, "Even Darcy Barnes is plastic. but you, Kelly Kimball are *not*. You're the real thing. REAL, girl!! Da real thang, G!!"

it cracks me up when tito gets all ghetto on me.

"Besides," he goes, "you're an aries and you were born

in the year of the tiger. what do you expect? you're a BORN superstar. you need to believe that. do you believe it?" I was like whatever. and he goes, "No, not WHATEVER. do you believe it or not?"

the way he was staring at me, boring into my eyes, was almost freaky and it made me believe him for a second. I go, ok yes. I believe it!

without taking his eyes off of mine or even blinking, he goes, ok, I think we're ready.

I was like, ready for what?

he goes, "Kelly, that t-shirt I brought you is special. it's for your audition tomorrow." then he reached into his cargo pocket, pulled out a flyer, and handed it to me. "You're going to be famous. Stop one on the fame train is tomorrow."

I looked down at the flyer. on one side was a silhouette of a girl who was like *jamming* in front of a bunch of bright stage lights. her hair was flying, and she looked like she was going THERE, too.

I flipped it over.

How REAL are you?

Wanted: FUTURE POP STARS!

We're looking for the fiercest, flyest, _REALEST_ females, ages 15–20, for all-new all-girl pop group. Must be able to dance, sing, and totally work it onstage. Be willing to show your belly. (Pierced belly buttons preferred but not required.)

Do YOU have what it takes? Be at SvenGali Studio, Santa Monica Blvd., Third Floor.

Friday May 24, 10 am. Ask for Don Dezer.

Have one dance routine and one song ready. Be prepared to stay all day. Bring the realness.

DON'T SHOW IF YOU CAN'T REPRESENT!

Out loud, I was like yeah RIGHT. we get these flyers in the dance studio all the time! but you never hear about anyone ever actually *going* to one. forget it tito. these things are bogus. but on the inside, I was like omigod could you imagine?

Tito was still staring at me. he was like no, I'm serious. how do you know it's bogus unless you go? besides I'll go with you.

"no way that sounds like the dumbest thing ever," I told him. but inside I was instantly tripping, hard.

DON'T SHOW IF YOU CAN'T REPRESENT!

I mean, hello!! I could represent! I mean, picture me at the audition . . . i would soooo be *representing.* so good (so REAL) they'd totally cancel plans for whatever random all-girl group and make me a solo act.

Kelly Kimball, Pop Star!

I could picture the whole thing. me onstage at some huge massive concert, like MTV Spring Break only bigger, and everyone totally chanting for me "Kel-LY! Kel-LY!" And get this—it's an all-star crowd. I could see

9

Nelly chanting for me. Britney Spears is there with Beyonce. I could see Pink. I could see Christina Aguilera (or is it Xtina now?). I could see Pashmina, the so-called Anti-Darcy, I could see Jesse Nixon with Justin Timberlake. (anyone feel like a sandwich?!) I could even see Darcy Barnes, *the* Darcy Barnes, shouting my name. I closed my eyes so I could hear them better. on that stage I was a universe away from my real life, my poor-ass self, evan, my delinquent brother, my crazy mother, my evil stepfather and his grotesque twin daughters. I was Kelly Kimball, pop star, and that's all I could see.

the studio phone rang somewhere in the background but I ignored it. I mean, this is a pretty good daydream here. In fact I have it a lot. I mean ALL THE TIME. even more than the one about the Jesse/Justin sandwich.

But that daydream is a fantasy. I go, Tito, we can't go. i have school tomorrow and so do you. it's not happening.

he goes, We're going.

I go, be serious, Tito. I don't even have a routine. are you crazy?

he goes, what do you call what you just did in there? I am telling you now that you were flawless.

you know, tito, I said, if we lived in LA we could go to auditions like this all the time, but we live in San Diego, which is too far away from SvenGali studios. thanks for the ego boost, though. I forced a smile.

Then Tito goes, I don't know what you're talking about.

10

we're going. I already arranged it. I'll pick you up at 6 AM. Our bus leaves at 6:15. I realized he was waving bus tickets in my face. I go, are you KIDDING?

he goes, I am so NOT kidding. then he stopped spinning. he goes, Kelly, this is your time. your dream could happen. but you have to let it happen.

I didn't say anything even though my mind was racing. I can't go. I can't go. why can't I go? what if I go, what could happen? I opened my mouth to talk a couple of times but couldn't come up with anything.

tito goes, Besides, think of the money.

the money.

it was then that I realized we really *were* going to LA to SvenGali Studios on the 6:15 bus. Tomorrow. I think I'll bring the Beatz laptop so I can write.

I need an altoid.

SVENGALI STUDIOS

LOS ANGELES, 11:15 AM

Outfit: orange cargo shorts (at the knee, not capris), Tito's cowboy t-shirt. sports bra, which is currently digging into my armpit. note: ass looks great in these shorts.

Hair: pulled underneath into my old Astros baseball cap.

Mood: need caffeine

Fortune: Eat a good breakfast.

---

omigod I think I've lost it. I'm crazy. am I crazy? I've definitely lost it.

no I haven't.

yes I have.

we're really here. I'm about to audition.

the bus trip was totally uneventful. tito and I split my headphones and listened to Dido. Tito was asleep for half the trip.

once we got there, my nerves calmed down. even though there was already a line of about a hundred girls up alongside this big warehouse, it looked at first glance like there was no competition.

the first few girls just looked like cheerleaders, some

12

looked like kind of pseudo-hip-hop-wannabe chicks. I noticed a couple of drama clubbers and at least one obvious beauty queen. a lot of the girls were trying to pretend they weren't there with their stage mothers. this one girl had this total poser goth thing going on— probably courtesy of the "goth" section at contempo casuals at her local mall. I overheard one girl talking to this other girl, telling her how she was from argentina. (Maybe that's why her boobs were so big. yeah, maybe.) anyway "lucky star" by Madonna came on and the argentinian girl started singing and dancing around, all hoochie-like but it sounded so funny cause she kept moaning like a porn star and going "ju mus' be mai lockey essstar." then the girl she was talking to started writhing around too. hello freak dancing. And then, omigod. they started moving toward each other and their heads ducked into each other and I was thinking no they aren't about to kiss but before I could even gasp or say omigod to tito, they totally kissed. I'm talking tongue and everything! I mean, it was sloppy. like a full-on TATU kiss. Spittle everywhere. Then they broke and went right back into their little dance like they'd choreographed it or something. Tito was like ok, Madonna and Britney. This is NOT the MTV awards. I was like oh man I hope for her sake they're not going to broadcast this back in Argentina.

anyway everyone was like stretching out and drinking vitamin water and chatting about shows they'd "done." (note: everyone on the audition circuit has "done" west side story or grease at least once.) there was a lot of lipgloss

13

being passed around and plenty of scales being sung. I put my headphones on to drown out the noise. Not to mention the illness.

tito eyed me with this look that said "you're a shoo-in" and I was feeling pretty confident.

halfway down the line we started noticing that there were, in fact, some pretty good dancers around. The ones that didn't feel like they had to arrive at the crack of dawn to make a good impression. these two girls halfway back through the line had on these really dope black bodysuits. they were stretching out and doing spins and looking really loose. there was this one macy-gray-looking chick who was singing along to this jill scott song that tito's always playing. her voice was incredible, like Alicia Keys meets mary j. blige. there was one girl who was there with like three adults . . . these two women in power suits and this guy in faded lucky jeans and a black t-shirt. all three of them were on cell phones. tito figured that was her management team or whatever. he called her "the pro." I started getting pretty intimidated.

when we settled into the back of the line, I took off my baseball cap to readjust my ponytail. tito gasped. Girl why didn't we color your hair last night? Your roots!

I glared at him. Thanks, Tito, I said. That makes me feel great. there's not much I can do about it now.

sorry! he goes. I'm just saying. Put your cap on.

just then, we noticed, about thirty people up the line, this man in a cheesy polo shirt and this woman in Lee Relaxed Fit Jeans and a fanny pack—walking down the line, pointing at certain people, tapping them on the shoulder, and saying "You" to them. they were only tapping, like, every third person or something. they kept coming closer, and tito and I looked at each other like oh SHIT they're typing people out—just sending them home if they don't have the right look. what if I don't get tapped?

That was the first time I really felt it. I wanted it, and I wanted it bad. and not only that, I had a feeling I could get it.

we held our breath as the polo shirt man and the fanny-pack woman got closer to us. my body stiffened up and my eyes glazed over. I stared into the distance, trying to avoid making eye contact with them. would they tap me? I felt my stomach tighten like a drum as they breezed up to me . . . and passed me right by.

they totally ignored me. no one pointed at me and said "You." I looked at tito, whose eyes were darting around the line trying to make sense of the scene.

luckily, we were close to the end of the line, so when polo and fanny got to the end of the line polo turned back to us and yells as loud as he could, "If we tapped your shoulder, please form another line over to the right, behind that blue door. if we didn't tap your shoulder, thank you very much and we hope to see you again."

I looked at tito. he looked at me. we both knew no one tapped my shoulder.

I took a step to leave when tito grabbed me around the waist and led me to the new line. I was like um, tito what are you doing? They didn't tap me. So Tito tapped my shoulder. "There, you're tapped. Get in the line."

I love tito.

anyway, everyone in the new line (there were about 30 of us now, including the girls in the black bodysuits, macy gray, the pro, and the argentinian) filed through the blue door into a huge room. it was like 5 times the size of beatz. we all sat on the floor when this guy got up to talk to us. his name was Don Dezer and I could smell his cologne from across the room and it wasn't good. he gave us this big speech about the group they were forming, Nice 'n Easy. they said they need attitude, energy, and realness. tito winked at me when he said that. See? he whispered. Realness. *Realness.* You got that.

after the speech they said that our "people" had to go. he meant the stage mothers, the managers, everyone. "the pro," who was sitting right behind us, gasped, loud. her handlers flitted around her, chirping it's ok, it's ok.

I turned to tito, who was laughing. he goes, I guess I'm your "people." I was like, you can't leave me. He smiled and said, "I'm here with you even if i'm not here with you. the t-shirt will bring you good luck, ok? I'll be at CaliBurger across the street. Remember, realness."

16

that was a half hour ago. Don Dezer just announced that vocal tests were about to begin and I just realized I've never been so nervous in my whole entire life.

it is taking every muscle in my body to keep me from racing out of here to join tito in the safety of the CaliBurger.

BUS STATION

LOS ANGELES, 5:22 PM

Hair: sensitive area, I'd rather not discuss. thanks to Tito.
Mood: don't ask

---

so here's how it played. No one seemed to notice that I was typed out. Which was awesome, but it meant I had to work extra hard to keep it that way. they had us do some really easy vocal tests in little groups, mostly just reading music, matching notes, stuff like that. it was really pretty simple stuff. I mean it's not like they were looking for a champion vocalist or anything. but even still, I was nervous and screwed up the first few bars. I asked to start again, took a deep breath, reminded myself that I've sung in front of 2,000 people before (at that a cappella competition in 10th grade . . . I came in 2nd), and more importantly, that worst-case scenario, I'd never see these people again, and gave it another shot. I sounded pretty good.

"The Panel," as they referred to themselves, were weird . . . they never gave anyone any feedback or anything. the five of them just sat there taking notes. it was like in that really old movie Flashdance. Don Dezer just kept saying "thank you, next" when people were done. I guess they were just trying to get rid of the totally tone deaf. I've been to a million trillion auditions before but

I'd never come across producers who were so cold before. they were just like pushing people out of there. they didn't push me out, though, which I figured was a good sign.

after the vocal tests, they told us they were taking a 5-minute break. I plugged my discman into my ears, lay down in the corner, closed my eyes, and listed to some darcy barnes. I went through the routine in my head a couple of times. it was solid, I really knew the moves. And like tito said, I pulled it off pretty well yesterday. I bet I could do it again.

45 minutes later I woke up—that kind of waking up where you didn't even realize you were asleep in the first place. I couldn't believe I'd fallen asleep. my head-phones were still on even though darcy barnes had way long ago stopped singing. I chugged the red bull that Tito had stuffed in my knapsack.

I realized all the girls were gathered around the door, where they posted a list of 20 names who would move on to the next level of the audition. the bodysuits were on there. macy gray. the pro. And yup, there was me: "Kimball, K." I needed another red bull.

They broke us up into two groups. my group went into another studio where don dezer and two of the other judges had set up a video camera.

the judges showed us a few routines and had us do them. none of them were that hard *at all* (even though I tripped over myself more than I would have if I had been dancing at home). most of it was stuff I learned in hip-hop class last fall. but there were no mirrors, which was really weird. I've almost never danced without a mirror. it's a lot harder. but even still I caught myself sliding THERE once or twice and improvising a little. I mean, not in an annoying overachiever way or anything, at least not as far as I'm concerned. I was just giving them some REALNESS, just like tito told me to.

the macy gray wannabe gave me a totally dirty look and it pissed me off. I really wished tito could be there right then.

anyway, they did another cut and there were just 10 of us left. me, the bodysuits, macy gray, the pro, and a few others. (not the argentinian. they sent her home after she came on to not one but two of the judges.) Anyway, I knew we were getting down to the wire, for real. it was time for our individual routines.

those two girls in the bodysuits went before me and even though they were dressed like they knew what they were doing, they both did these surprisingly dorky dances, like something they'd learned in a funk aerobics class together or something. the judges gave them no reaction, just a thank you, you're free to go, we'll post our decision after 6, next please. macy gray stepped up and threw down a disco routine, which she was obviously really into because she was throwing herself around like some freak in a good charlotte video. but it was obviously not very well choreographed. I wondered what the judges would think of her, but again, no reaction.

then it was my turn. all eyes on me. including macy gray, who had gone back to scowling at me.

I wasn't exactly sure how I was doing. I mean, I think I was pretty good. I mean, I don't know. I definitely hit all the steps and was on tempo and everything, but I felt a little stiff. I kept looking up, and because there were no mirrors I'd get stuck on seeing that macy gray's mean look and I couldn't get THERE.

but I finished, on cue and on balance. as far as I could tell, I'd done ok.

no reaction from the judges. don dezer was just writing stuff in his notebook and futzing with the video camera. he goes, "thank you Miss . . . um . , . uh . . . Kimball, yes. you're free to go. we will post our decision after 6. next?"

then it happened. the pro girl went right after me, took the center of the floor, and waited for her music. halfway through the first beat, I knew I was in trouble. this girl was dancing to darcy barnes!!

and not only that, she was doing the EXACT SAME routine that I did! I couldn't believe it. I watched her like a hawk. was she better than me? worse? is this good for me? bad? am I screwed? I kept looking to the judges for any reaction, any sign, any emotion in their stony faces.

the song was over fast, and I concluded that I did just as well as the pro.

no reaction from the judges.

I was starving. I went to find tito at the CaliBurger. I needed the biggest double double cheeseburger ever made. I hadn't eaten all day and I was STARVING! I told tito I didn't want to talk I just wanted to eat. he totally understood.

after scarfing for a half hour I looked up to see Don Dezer and two other members of the panel walk over and take the booth right behind us. they didn't see me, thank god, but I could totally hear them talking. I gave tito the "shhh" signal and listened to Dezer and his crew, who were in mid-conversation:

"What about that Kimball girl?"

"She's good on the floor and her voice is ok but there's nothing original about her. She's a poser. she's not REAL at all. she's a clone. everything she did was a darcy barnes ripoff and that's the last thing we need."

"she's good, though."

"yeah she's good but she's not very real."

"yeah you're right. she's a darcy barnes clone. Strike her off the list."

"Ok, Kelly's off. So we have Tracy, Thelma, Roni, and Dale. We still need a fifth."

"Well, our fifth definitely isn't here today. We'll have to hold more auditions. Go put up the list."

tito and I just stared at each other in shock with our mouths open. a bite of burger actually fell out of my mouth onto its paper wrapping. I wanted really bad to crack up with tito right now and laugh at ourselves, laugh at how silly the whole day had been, laugh at the other girls who'd been auditioning, laugh at Don Dezer's cologne, laugh at the burger falling out of my mouth, laugh at the humiliation of it all. But the humiliation didn't feel funny right away. I felt like a complete loser. I mean, the ONE thing I thought I had to offer, the one thing tito said I had, was some so-called realness, and they didn't get that at all. Not to mention that they compared me to darcy barnes, which would have been exactly what I wanted five minutes ago, but now it sucked. tito grabbed his backpack. "c'mon, we are totally out of here." he stood up and walked around to my side of the booth, grabbed my arm, and went, really loud, "let's go!" I wonder if "The Panel" heard him.

we took off. we didn't even bother to wait until after six to go up to the studio to see some stupid list without my name on it. we just raced back to the bus station. tito kept going off about how they don't know what they're talking about and they don't even know what real is and blah blah blah until I had to tell him to shut up.

he just showed me the new Darcy Barnes milk mustache ad in US Weekly. I grabbed it out of his hand and tore it up. I'm so not a clone of her.

MY ROOM, 9:59 AM (And I'm not coming out. except maybe for ice cream.)

Outfit: cloud pj bottoms and one of dad's old tees.
Hair: haven't checked.
Fortune: you can't step in the same river twice.

---

by the time I got home it was almost 2. way after curfew but it's not like it's the first time I've snuck in after curfew. I was brushing my teeth when staci came into the bathroom to pee. I was like great, she'll probably tell. but she looked half asleep so I figured she wouldn't remember.

when I got up I was seriously bummed.

I mean, not that I really really wanted to get picked or anything, it's just, well, I don't know. I wish I'd been able to say no to THEM, instead of the other way around. kinda like how it's better to be the one who does the dumping instead of the one who gets dumped.

I signed on and Evan IMed me from the basement. he got to move to the basement last week when he turned 15 and finished his community service sentence (300 hours of picking up trash) and get this: his parole officer's wife, this software executive or something, gave evan an old computer from her office that they were throwing out. I think it was for like some outreach to troubled teens program or something.

Anyway, it's gross down there in the basement. I can't figure out why he'd want to move there. god only knows what he does down there. ew. boys are retarded.

his latest IM name is **SlipKnotRules933111**. he can't even get our zip code right. freak.

SlipKnotRules933111: are you up

KellyKelSoCal321: dude I'm online. I'm up

SlipKnotRules933111: staci or traci or one of them said you were out all night

KellyKelSoCal321: no way. I didn't think her little nine-year-old brain would remember. If she even has one.

SlipKnotRules933111: well, she did. Knowing her, she probably ran straight to carl.

KellyKelSoCal321: ugh. carl just LOVES busting me. why did mom have to marry him? he's so annoying. whatever. it wasn't that late. I was in LA. Staci would spontaneously combust if she knew what I was doing.

SlipKnotRules933111: ha ha what were you doing

KellyKelSoCal321: nothing. auditioning to be in a pop group. it was stupid.

SlipKnotRules933111: well, you missed the best scariest police videos last night

KellyKelSoCal321: are you sure you're allowed to watch that? I mean dude, you're still in the system. shouldn't you be confined to only watching the Disney Channel or something? lol. wait . . . Mom's at my door.

KellyKelSoCal321: ok I'm back. she's like where were you last night and I was like hanging out with tito (which is totally true)

SlipKnotRules933111: wait she's yelling down the stairs. what does she WANT? she probably hasn't taken her medication yet today

KellyKelSoCal321: that's not funny evan. depression is a real disease. I looked it up. and you know she doesn't want us to know about it.

SlipKnotRules933111: whatever.

KellyKelSoCal321: how is school anyway

SlipKnotRules933111: this week we're doing "Anger Management" and "Taking Responsibility" and stuff but whatever.

KellyKelSoCal321: when are you out for the summer

SlipKnotRules933111: we aren't. delinquents like me stay in school all year. that's why carl hates me . . . my special education is too "expensive."

KellyKelSoCal321: ha ha. carl just hates me for the fun of it. dude I made it to the final round yesterday at the audition in LA. I was almost in a group! but then they cut me.

SlipKnotRules933111: what group. what are you talking about.

KellyKelSoCal321: in LA dipstick. I just told you. a new pop group.

SlipKnotRules933111: like on that TV show? and you blew it?

KellyKelSoCal321: that's a really nice way to say it. thanks a lot.

KellyKelSoCal321: hello?

KellyKelSoCal321: DUDE?

SlipKnotRules933111: sorry i'm downloading. quit calling me dude.

KellyKelSoCal321: whatever I'm signing off

SlipKnotRules933111: i bet you were too good or something and that's why they had to vote you off. ha ha.

KellyKelSoCal321: like i'm so good everyone else would look bad? awww. thanks dude. I think. :-) don't play with matches. later sk8r.

I worry about the kid sometimes. I mean, he doesn't have much in the way of a role model. Dad's been gone for over eight years, and mom, well, the best I can say is that she thinks she does her best. I don't know if she's ever gotten over losing dad. it was pretty sad the other night when I heard her humming to herself in the kitchen. it was "California Dreamin'" by this old group The Mamas and the Papas . . . and I realized she was crying. Which of course made me cry too.

that was dad's signature song. actually, it was our favorite song together. he sang melody and he taught me the harmony and we sounded pretty good. I think about that sometimes before I sleep.

mom also thinks she needs a man to get by, but I'm not sure how being with carl, who smells like farts and watches the Golf Channel all weekend every weekend, is better than being alone.

and don't even get me started on Staci and Traci, carl's twin daughters. between their 22 pageant titles (from Little Miss Junior Citrus San Diego to America's Junior Twinkle–Miss West or whatever) and their refusal to wear any shoes without taps, they are truly, deeply evil and must be stopped. if anyone gets this diary and I've been killed, they did it.

the thing is evan's a really good kid. really smart. but when he doesn't have someone telling him what to do, he comes up with really bad ideas. like burning down organic markets.

Well, I better go brush my teeth. I never get why they taste gross in the morning. I mean I brushed them before i went to bed and it's not like i'm eating pizza in my sleep but whatever.

MY ROOM, 9:24 PM

Outfit: sports bra and basketball shorts
Hair: shiny, but smells a little like avocado from this treatment tito gave me yesterday.
Mood: recovered.
Fortune: Know you.

I went on a great run this morning with evan and it kind of helped me sweat out the last day or two.

evan is starting to get really fast these days—he can totally out-mile me back to back. he made me sing the whole time tho—he loves making me do that. it's cool. I mean i guess it's good for my voice. Anyway, i'm totally over that whole pop star thing. Don Dezer and the rest of them are all completely clueless and don't know real-ness when they see it.

I'm not Nice 'n Easy anyway. I'm Kelly Kimball. I have my pride. I have my identity. and I have finals this week.

SCHOOL, STUDY HALL, 11:14 AM

Outfit: tech skirt and pullover hoodie. I know, it's kinda last year but whatever.
Hair: should I get bangs?
Mood: I hate myself. But I hate you more.
Fortune: Play it as it lays.

How much do I hate my current life? Let me count the ways:

1. I have three finals and an English paper to do this week.

2. I am exhausted. I was up until 2:30 last night trying to understand what said paper is supposed to be about. (Apparently I've spent the last semester enrolled in a class called "Character Motivations in the Novel and Short Story Forms" and didn't even know it.) Then I got woken up at 5:45 this morning when the freak twins Staci and Traci started practicing their pageant rendition of this old Whitney Houston song "I Wanna Dance with Somebody." It makes them sound like Alvin and the Chipmunks singing destiny's child. it's not good.

3. Carl, my stepfather.

4. I am still 24 hours from my period and have never been bitchier.

i only slept an hour last night. i'm in that kind of mood where everything just seems so ridiculous or hopeless or something that all you can do is laugh at all of it. mom calls it "punchy." stuff that on normal days would kinda freak me out seemed funny to me today. Like, "I blew that European history exam! i'm probably gonna get a D in the class! ha ha ha" or "my mom likes my stepsisters better than she likes me! ha ha ha!" or "I weigh five pounds more than I did yesterday."

Whatever. I'm gonna go see if we have phish food in the freezer. Later.

THURSDAY MAY 30

MY ROOM, 4 PM

Outfit: Um lemme look. ok jeans and a Roxy tee.
Hair: I'd give it a 6.5 out of ten.
Mood: freaking
Fortune: Don't overthink.

Omigod Omigod Omigod.

I'm freaking out. ok I can't believe it. I'm going back to LA. To audition again. not another audition for pop stars. this time I'm auditioning for darcy barnes. let me rephrase. DARCY BARNES WANTS TO MEET ME AND SEE ME DANCE.

ok ok ok. ok don't panic. ok.

this is just totally too weird. isn't it? I mean, how did this happen? how many millions of times have I listened to her cds? how many hours have I spent learning her routines in front of my bedroom mirror? How many times have I uttered her name? (how many times have I totally dissed her outfits with tito while flipping through Teen People?) and now I'm going to be meeting her . . . and DANCING for her!

ok ok ok I'm getting ahead of myself. here's what happened. I got home after school (biology exam was multiple choice! whew!!) and signed on to check my email. there was this random one:

To: Kel_Kimball
From: EileenW_hitpatrol
Date: Thursday May 30
Time: 10:38 AM
Subject: Dance opportunity for you

You don't know me, but my name is Eileen Wang. I'm the tour manager for Darcy Barnes's *It's Darcy!!* tour. My friend Don Dezer, who manages the Pop-Tarts, showed me a tape of your audition last Friday, and although I understand you weren't selected for that job, I'm very interested in talking to you about another, much bigger opportunity. I need you to be in LA this Saturday at 10 AM. Please email me back as soon as possible to confirm.
Eileen Wang

I practically hyperventilated. These are the things I thought, in the order that I thought them. (I think.) Ok:

1. Who's messing with me?

2. How can I play this and get back at them, whoever it is?

3. there's no way this is for real.

4. could this be for real?

5. what if it's for real and I tell off Darcy Barnes's manager by mistake?

I stopped myself from thinking too hard. I was FREAK-ING OUT. I decided to be professional, just in case it wasn't a joke. I replied to the email right away (I sent it to tito first so he could check and make sure it was written correctly. He's always on me for not using proper grammar and punctuation.) "Hello. I am very interested in this opportunity but I do not know if I can be in LA on Saturday. Please call me." then I wrote my phone number.

anyway, she called me. I don't have time to write it all now because I have to go talk to tito, but it was totally FOR REAL. this woman eileen wants me to audition on saturday for a backup dancer spot on this summer's Darcy Barnes tour. at least I think that's what she said. it seems weird because it's kind of late to be auditioning for a summer tour, considering summer starts in like a couple of weeks. I know I have work and everything but whatever, I can just tell them I'm sick. I don't care. there's probably no way it would ever work out but so what I get to meet darcy barnes and dance for her OMIGOD how crazy is THAT?!

this is better than the pop star thing. way better. way, way better.

guess Eileen is looking for some REALNESS after all! ha ha. :-)

oh man I just realized. What's mom gonna say? i hope she lets me do it. But what if she doesn't? Ugh. can't think about that now. I gotta call tito. oh wait he can't talk on the phone. I gotta get over there!!

I cannot screw this up. I cannot, cannot, cannot, cannot, cannot screw this up. I cannot screw this up. how am I going to get to LA?

and what am I going to wear?

HOME, 8:45 PM

Outfit: dad's old cashmere sweater. it's getting all holey but I'll wear it forever. and gray track pants.
Mood: overdrive. I can't focus on anything. all I can think about is meeting darcy and not screwing up royally
Fortune: There is no free ride.

Ok. first of all, can I say thank god that trig exam was easyish because I didn't study at all last night. And SCHOOL'S OUT!! (I mean except for the junior picnic next monday and another makeup day for that day we got off for the earthquake last march. or was it last December. I can't remember anymore. but I mean, come ON. the junior picnic? I don't THINK so.)

now the bigger news: I'm definitely going to the audition. i have actually convinced Mom to drive me to LA tomorrow. It worked out really well because she has to take evan to go see this lawyer in the San Fernando Valley, which is like a half hour from LA. this lawyer dude might be able to get evan's probation shortened. which it should be. I mean, he hasn't burned anything down since that co-op. at least not that we know of. the kid needs a break.

I wonder if she'd be as easygoing about the audition if she weren't having so much trouble with carl. I mean, she seems totally out of it today. she and carl got into a huge fight last night. I guess he ended up sleeping in front of the tv because I came down to watch power-puff girls at 11:30 but I couldn't because he was snoring away. and it smelled like farts. loser.

maybe she's only ok with me trying out because she doesn't think I have a chance. I wonder if she'd actually let me go if I got it? It's Darcy!

anyway tito came by the dance studio today to help me practice my routines for tomorrow. the thing is, though, he was being really harsh on me. He gets that way, all perfectionist(ic?) and everything. he kept telling me I needed to get THERE. I was like, I can't just go there on command and I can't fake it. he goes, It shows. I go, That's mean. he goes, "Aries need to be reined in every now and then, and they need to be told the hard truth sometimes."

but I think maybe he's a little jealous too. he would love to dance for Darcy Barnes. but I love him and I know he loves me. and, well, whatever . . . we made a couple of improvements to the "Love You Like a Lollipop" routine.

HOME, MIDNIGHT

Outfit: low-rise sweats, pink tank
Mood: can't tell, too nervous about tomorrow

I hopped onto the internet to counter the full-on nervousness I'm feeling about tomorrow. tito called me Nervous Nelly earlier.

so it's going to be a family affair tomorrow . . . me, mom, AND evan.

SlipKnotRules933111: Dude what time do we leave tomorrow

KellyKelSoCal321: 9:30. Do Not, repeat, Do Not make us late.

SlipKnotRules933111: **shut up it's not like I want to be late either.**

KellyKelSoCal321: sorry dude no need for bold just harshin on you

SlipKnotRules933111: what are you going up there for anyway

KellyKelSoCal321: I already told you I'm auditioning for Darcy Barnes!

SlipKnotRules933111: who?

KellyKelSoCal321: Darcy BARNES! she's like a huge star.

SlipKnotRules933111: You mean like Britney Spears?

KellyKelSoCal321: Uh, no. oh forget it. you are so clueless.

SlipKnotRules933111: did you see Americas most wanted

KellyKelSoCal321: no

SlipKnotRules933111: it was good it was this guy who dissolved these kids in acid. by the way have you noticed mom and carl

KellyKelSoCal321: a little. why?

SlipKnotRules933111: well get this mom told me that after we meet with that lawyer dude for my thing that she has to talk to him alone about something else too. but she won't tell me what for.

KellyKelSoCal321: dude that could be nothing. She's probably doing something for carl

SlipKnotRules933111: I think not. I heard mom screaming at him about someone at work he's supposedly doing.

KellyKelSoCal321: WHAT

SlipKnotRules933111: yeah I don't know what's up but they haven't been speaking for like two days and he's going away with the twins for the weekend.

KellyKelSoCal321: well that's good at least. silence for once.

SlipKnotRules933111: I guess. see you in the morning. ok bye. ps if you want me to be on time you better come wake me up he signed off before I could bust on him for that.

ok, now any prayer I had for falling asleep was ruined. now I have to worry about the audition. And about mom getting all divorced again. I hate it when she's single . . . we're always so poor when she's single. I mean the last thing I want is to go back to sharing a room with Evan in a stupid little apartment somewhere, like when we lived above that house after dad died.

Uggh! I need to NOT worry about this right now. evan probably got it wrong. I need to relax. I need to sleep.

have I mentioned that I'm going to meet DARCY BARNES tomorrow? if i get this spot, I'm so out of here. see ya later San Diego. so long, double jonbenets and your farty father.

God I'm nervous.

SATURDAY JUNE 1 (I think. It could be Sunday morning, June 2. It's LATE.)

BACK HOME

Outfit: boys' briefs and a cami (just about to crash)
Fortune: I totally forgot to check today!!

I DID IT!!!!!!!! I FUCKING DID IT!!!!!! I'm a backup dancer on the IT'S DARCY!! tour!!!!!! I TOTALLY RULE!!!!

ok, I am way too tired to go into all the details. all I can say is I can't wait to tell tito how I saw darcy barnes applying little round band-aids to her nipples so they wouldn't show through her unitard. i guess it works but it's gotta suck when you rip 'em off. i bet it's gotta suck even harder when you have pierced nipples. I'm not saying that Darcy does. OK, yes I am.

as soon as I got back home and into my bedroom, I called tito on his cell phone, which he sleeps with on "vibrate."

He told me I was amazing and that I'd have to come over tomorrow and tell him all about it. I could tell he was really tired, but not too tired to ask if I met darla?

Darla. Ha. tito's obsessed with her. he's always obsessed with the weirdest people. like instead of being a celine dion fan he's totally focused on Rene, her husband. he was the first person I knew who had ever heard of willa ford.

anyway, darla is darcy's mother. And she's well known

41

because darcy barely makes a move without darla moving right alongside her. like it tones down her hoochiness or something. like if her own mother doesn't have a problem with darcy practically stripping onstage, then the rest of the world will be cool with it, too. I mean, people think Pashmina is way sluttier . . . I wonder if it's because her mother is never around. I mean, they both do the thong-with-chaps look, only for some reason it just looks nastier on Pashmina. I don't get it.

anyway I wouldn't know what darla's really like because I didn't meet darla. so I said, "I didn't meet darla."

so then Tito goes, "Are they real?" and I knew he was talking about her boobs. I go, "I don't know but all I'm saying is they don't really move. I mean, they move, but they don't *move*. that makes sense, right? anyway darcy borrowed my belly button ring."

ew, I hope you purelled, said tito.

call me when you wake up, I go. or I'll call you. that's all for now. i'll fill you in on all the fabulosity tomorrow.

MY ROOM, 3 PM

Outfit: I'm trying to pack so I've been doing costume changes for the last hour. I wonder how many shoes I'll need. good thing I'll be making plenty of cash. I can buy new shoes in every city!
Hair: ponytail, high and sloppy
Mood: so, so psyched.
Fortune: Begin at the beginning.

---

tito and I spent the morning out back in his yard putting tea in our hair. it's supposed to make it shiny or something. we didn't know what kind of tea to use so we just made nestea iced tea and poured it on our heads. no lemon tho. we learned the Sun-In lesson YEARS ago.

the first thing he said was, How much are you going to make?

and I said, way more than enough. trust me.

tito wiped a fake tear from his cheek. he goes, My baby's going to be rich. come here, come give me a hug.

I did.

then I filled him in on all of yesterday's details. and as dad would have said, "it went a little something like THIS:"

the whole time we drove up to LA evan and mom were arguing about how he has to stay in school all summer long. i kinda felt bad for him but i agree with her. I mean he messed up big time so he really should stick to the rules for a while. he knows it, too. he's just whining.

anyway they dropped me off at this random studio in Santa Monica. Eileen had emailed me the address. the door was totally locked and there was no buzzer or anything. I knew I wasn't late so I told mom and evan to just leave and just sat on my backpack and scarfed down the second powerbar of the morning. I was, as tito's mother always says, *nerviosa!*

My level of nervousness for the pop stars audition was nothing compared to this. I sat on that curb for what felt like hours.

I didn't have my watch on me and I left my cellie in the car so I had no idea what time it was. what if I got the wrong day? what if they changed their minds? what if this was all a practical joke after all?

i was about to get up and leave when this cool-looking asian woman with spiked hair, black jeans, a leather blazer, and square glasses starts screaming, "Kelly? Kelly Kimball! Hey! Kelly! Whasssup Kelly! Woo-hoo!"

I was like whoa! who is that and how does she know me?

she came closer. she started talking, really really really fast. Like a cartoon. "I'm so psyched you made it! I was seriously bumming out when shania . . . that's the backup dancer you're replacing . . . well auditioning to replace . . . shania tore three ligaments on tuesday night and even though we tried really hard to get her to dance on wednesday she just kept falling over and even when we told her that we can't do the show without her and we were all depending on her and that this is just a really really inconvenient time for her to get injured and everything she just kept collapsing and everything . . . then when the orthopedic surgeon told us that she needed surgery asap and she wouldn't be recovered for four months . . . I got into a serious panic because I mean It's Darcy!! starts in just a couple of weeks, really, and to calm me down my boyfriend don dezer . . . I call him diseazer but the thing is . . . he showed me this tape of all these really bad girls who auditioned for him last weekend but then when you came on and we watched your routine I was like holy toledo that's sha- nia! and he was like no it's not and I was like I know you dick but I need this girl she's just as good as shania but younger, which really matters, gimme her number . . . and he said he didn't have your number anyway that's when I emailed you and you came here and thank god you're here and look at you you're perfect and come upstairs and darla's going to love you."

or something like that. I was just like: Wow. *I* needed to take a breath after that.

then she goes, "I'm eileen. Eileen Wang. sorry. nice to meet you. the job pays $40,000 for the summer plus expenses. would that be acceptable?"

"Ok!" I said, unable to think, just respond. "and nice to meet you, too!" I realized I was almost yelling. Forty thousand dollars was more than anyone in my family had ever seen at one time.

From there, the next four hours were a daze. Eileen took me up to this studio and told me to get warmed up. it was really bright in there cause the sun was shining like directly into the windows. well it wasn't really windows more like a wall that was glass. the whole rest of the room was surrounded by mirrors. I was in there for a while by myself and I started tripping out that they were those two-way kind of mirrors (the kind that they always tell you department stores have in their dressing rooms so you supposedly won't be tempted to shoplift but really you just get nervous that someone's seeing you in your underwear . . . you know those).

$40,000!!!

Anyway, Eileen came in a couple of minutes later. she goes, "behind those mirrors over there darcy and a couple of the dancers are hanging out. I've already shown them the tape of your routine for 'Love You Like a Lollipop' which she totally loved I mean she said it totally rocked. so now they're having cappuccino fro yos and Kozy Shacks and they want to watch you do the routine in person. I hope it doesn't freak you out too much that they're back there . . . does it? is it too weird? you can tell me if it's too weird."

weird? what do i know from weird? when's the last time I had to audition for the biggest MTV star in the universe? maybe this is just how it worked. it totally

46

freaked me out though. I mean I started thinking maybe there were like 40 people back there, all with clipboards and stuff, looking really mean. but I was like KELLY suck it up and deal this is IT. ok, fine. if it's two-way mirrors, it's two-way mirrors. "no problem," I said, scrounging up a smile. or at least trying to.

"great ok I'll go cue up your music if you're ready." she closed the door behind her, and the door kind of melted into the mirror so much that after a while I kind of forgot where the door was. I was TOTALLY tripping out at this point. I knew all these people were watching but all I could see was reflections of myself. it seemed crowded in there, but it was only me. I was truly, schooly freaking out. "ok, sure," I said.

this is it, I kept thinking, this is it. don't blow it. you've done this a thousand times so don't think about it. breathe. breathe. I heard Eileen over a speaker (I never figured out where the speakers were . . .) "ok, um, all set, Kelly?"

i nodded. i heard the first few beats (luckily i'd built in a two-bar pause at the top of the routine so I couldn't be caught off guard) and felt my legs start to move. it was strange not knowing where to focus because they could have been behind any of those walls. Luckily I also realized that if I tried to see through the glass, to see behind it, I'd look like a real idiot. I got that from watching the real world. so I just picked a spot to center myself with and stuck with it.

as soon as the song hit the first chorus, though, the music stopped. "um, sorry, Kelly. hey, um . . . the girls weren't watching. would you mind starting over?"

I didn't know which way the voice was coming from or where I was supposed to look when I answered it so I just said, "SURE NO PROB." that got me flustered, but I kept it under control. I kept thinking about the way tito would react if I screwed up. he'd glare at me in horror, then pretend that darcy barnes had no idea what she was doing and that she was a moron for not choosing me and that I'd be a star no matter what and did I want to deep-condition anything. I wasn't sure I could take all that, so I was determined not to screw up.

and we started again. this time I figured I had find to find my way THERE—as soon as possible. and stay THERE.

luckily I found it. in fact, once the music started again, it wrapped me up like a spring roll. i was flying, working, striking, hitting EVERYTHING in a way that I've never felt. I just went for it and rocked. it was like how when you know someone important is watching you, you kick everything up a notch (either that or you totally collapse and fall apart. luckily that didn't happen this time). anyway it felt like a total "peak" as Danielle my ballet teacher used to call it.

except right as I was "peaking" the music conked out. silence. I just looked around at myself (myselves) in the mirror.

I stood there, still breathing, not sure what to do. I realized I'd raced from sitting outside on the curb to auditioning for darcy barnes to waiting for a response and forgetting which way I was facing in the space of only 10 minutes. this was all happening so fast, even if for a moment it felt like nothing at all was happening.

there goes the $40,000, I thought.

still nothing.

then the mirror cracked. cracked open. I fixed my eyes on the floor in front of where the mirror opened into the room. I was too scared to look up. I was expecting eileen wang to step out of the mirror-door and tell me to go home. This was bad.

slowly I raised my gaze, hoping that perhaps eileen would come out and again tell me that they weren't watching.

and out popped darcy barnes! it was so unreal. like, this girl I've seen 100,000 pictures of, whose wardrobe I know even better than my own, was all of a sudden right there in front of my face! she looked different . . . not like different different, but the expression she had on her face was kind of, I don't know, unglamorous. and she had a zit on her chin! And she was taller than I thought. all these things went whipping through my head, and what do I say? omiGOD you're Darcy Barnes!

Then I wondered whether I was even allowed to talk to her. Or whether I was supposed to do something to show my respect, like curtsy.

"hi!" she goes. "I *looove* your tank!"

that's what she said when she hired me. not "You were great!" or "Sweet moves" or "It will take a lot of work but you'll probably do OK. Nope. just "I *looove* your tank!"

made me wonder whether my dancing had anything to do with it. what if I'd worn a different tank?

tito was like, How do you spell the way she said "looove" and I go, I'm pretty sure you spell it with three O's. at least.

MY ROOM, MIDNIGHT

Outfit: I have changed over 30 times today and I still don't know what to wear tomorrow. oh, and there's the little issue of packing for the next three months away from home.

Mood: should I be a little sadder that I'm leaving for the summer? maybe, but I'm too excited.

---

other than tito, evan, mom, and the dance studio (they were pissed, not that I really cared. I mean, hello $40,000!), I haven't told anyone about my summer plans. Tito's the only friend I hang out with anyway. The rest of them will find out through the grapevine or something. besides, as soon as darcy barnes said, "I looove your tank!!" my entire focus has been on leaving tomorrow.

evan hasn't spoken to me since the car ride home yesterday. after I told him that I got an offer from the It's Darcy!! people, he basically ignored me. I guess that's just his way. he doesn't want me to go and this is his way of telling me. dude is pretty sensitive. anyway he was there when I signed on for the last time from home.

SlipKnotRules933111: can you give me a ride to OzzFest on Wednesday?

KellyKelSoCal321: evan. I won't be here. I told you. I'm leaving tomorrow.

SlipKnotRules933111: ok

KellyKelSoCal321: i'm sorry. i'm going to miss you a lot

SlipKnotRules933111: whatever. it's not like I need you for a ride anyway. i'm not helpless. it's not like I have some walkathon disease or anything.

Then he signed off.

I'm worried about him. The only thing he has going for him at the moment is that martino "corrective" school for ex-con teens he's in. turns out he's like a genius. the kid's already finished 11th grade physics, and he got an A. I got a D, barely. he's going to start taking college classes next year in architecture. one day an arsonist, the next an architect. go figure. I guess they understand him there. which is good cause nobody else seems to.

the only thing about the Martino School is the cost. it's way more than we can afford. Carl paid for the semester that Evan took last year, and he never lets any of us forget it. I would love it if we didn't have to take his money.

speaking of money, did I mention that I'll be making a couple of bucks this summer? or, I mean, $40,000 for three months!!!???!!?!?! sorry, I guess I already mentioned that.

anyway I think i'll save some money for evan. it could help free up my mom to get out of this carl situation.

I'm crashing now. Eileen said there was a car coming tomorrow at 10 AM to take me to LA. a car? how about a jet? ha ha. just kidding I'm not that much of a diva. YET. ha ha.

52

ON THE WAY TO LA, 11:30 AM

Outfit: track pants, evan's Insane Clown Posse tee (not that I'm a fan or anything but for some reason I feel brave in it)
Hair: tito gave me braids last night so I just left 'em in.
Mood: a little weepy. I just left home. trying to be brave but, well, kinda weepy.
Fortune: Welcome luck whenever it appears.

The car came for me this morning at 10. i think that was the first time evan got that i was actually going. he came up from the basement, stuck his head out the garage door, goes "bye," then turned around and went back in. i feel really bad. but he'll be ok. plus I have my laptop so we'll definitely talk.

thank god the twins were at their pre-tween modeling class when I left. carl was watering the bushes out front. I heard him yell, "where's she going?" just before I slammed the door.

Mom is the only one who actually walked me to the car. she loves to take moments like these and pretend she's in a Lifetime made-for-television movie. she took a little breath. then exhaled. I didn't know if she was going to say something or just keep staring. her eyes kept darting back and forth. it was obvious she didn't know what to do. it was like she was waiting for me to say something meaningful, wise, hopeful, or something. I'm like hi, I don't have a team of writers like they do on life-time. and guess what I don't need the pressure!

the best I could think of was, "bye mom."

then she really went for it. she was whimpering, like, "ok baby. Go. Go because you CAN. I love you. I'll always be watching. i've never stopped watching every-thing you do, I never will. now, go."

she smiled but it was one of those moms-only "I want you to think that I don't want you to see it but really I do want you to see that I'm dying on the inside smiles." but it wasn't just for effect . . . I could tell it was hard for her. isn't it weird how you find yourself in those moments sometimes and you feel like it's not real, and you can't help thinking that what the other person is saying is totally cheesy? and then, like, later, after the moment's waaay gone, out of the blue, you realize how much it affected you or whatever and you start to bawl like a "Baby-Wails-a-Lot" doll?

that happened to me like 10 minutes ago. I mean I didn't really start to BAWL, but i'm kinda sniffly and weepy at the moment. when I began to cry the driver turned up the radio on this awful country station. I think he was trying to get out of asking "what's wrong?" which is fine with me cause I didn't want to talk to him about it anyway.

I just kept thinking what mom said: "Go because you can." like, kinda saying I'm old enough to handle it, smart enough to deal, talented enough to succeed, all that stuff. it's weird to realize how much it matters to me that my MOM would think that about me, that she trusts me, that she believes in me or something.

so here we are, on the way. Clay Aiken is blasting into my ears and it hurts. god I hope I remembered my disc-man. I need some sarah mclachlan and a nap . . .

WAIT! PANIC! I just had a horrible thought. What if everyone on the It's Darcy!! tour hates me?

There goes my nap with Sarah McL.

DARCY'S HOUSE (or as everyone here calls it, "D-Zone")

LOS ANGELES, 11:54 PM

Outfit: official It's Darcy!! concert tour tee (white on black), basketball shorts
Hair: they want me blonder. fine with me.
Mood: wiped out. been trying to keep my head down and do everything right. so far no major mess-ups. but no one's really being nice to me. I can't tell if they all hate me, but there sure have been a lot of staredowns.
Fortune: No one knows you better than you.

I am so tired I can't tell my ass from my elbow anymore. I've met more people in two days than I'd ever met before in my life. dancers, backup singers, managers, agents, drivers, bodyguards . . . it's insane. I'm exhausted. where do I begin?

for starters, eileen told me yesterday that I had to change my name.

so from now on i'm officially K.K. Darcy and everyone thinks K.K. sounds more "REAL" than Kelly. I guess the fact that it's not my real name doesn't really matter.

I'm still not sure if that means I'm K.K. Kimball or just K.K. I guess I'll have to check the program.

whatever, i'm cool with it. most of the dancers seem to have nicknames. I probably would have picked something else, but what am I going to do, argue about it and lose the job?

so after getting up at 8 (we each share a room with another dancer but I have a room to myself because I'm new, I guess), all the dancers did a stretching class for an hour, then a pilates/core strength class for an hour. I didn't realize that stuff could be so tough. I was ready for a break.

except we didn't get one. darcy emerged from her suite at 10:30 AM, and we started rehearsing. and we didn't finish until 11 PM.

no one was really MEAN to me, but no one was really NICE to me either. I mean, i'm not sure exactly how I did (everything went so fast), and every routine was totally 100% new to me so I never got THERE (or anywhere near it), but at least I don't remember totally embarrassing myself anywhere along the way. I guess, I don't know. And like I said, there were plenty of stares. But no glares, at least. There is a difference.

darcy barely spoke to me once. in fact she barely spoke to anyone at all. not in a mean way or anything, just like it was all work. Everything they say about her working seriously hard is true. I didn't notice it so much at the audition, but when she does speak, it's in this like texas but valley girl kind of accent. kinda low but still really young. like, "omylordy y'all! I'm gagging" and stuff like that. it was kind of weird when I realized that she doesn't talk to anyone, especially considering how nice she was the other day at my audition, but I guess the pro in her is all about work.

I don't know what is going on with the rest of the dancers. you always see like Janet Jackson and people like that on tv talking about how they're all best friends with their dancers and how everyone's like some kind of big happy family or whatever. but it sure didn't seem that way. part of me assumed it was just me that didn't fit in. but by the end of today it started to look like no one was really getting along.

I am SO missing tito right now. he'd know what to do to break the ice. and if he couldn't break the ice at least we'd be able to bug out together.

my best bet for a friend looks like the choreographer, Rashid. he's really really cool. he told me I have excellent instincts but also a big job ahead of me. he said he'd help me out after hours and stuff if I needed it. he was asking me all about my body, about injuries I've had, what my strengths are as a dancer, what my weaknesses are, stuff like that. he seems like he really cares about all the dancers a lot, and he knows EVERYTHING about them. he winked when he said "everything."

After rehearsals one of the Men in Black took all the dancers to Mas Macho Taco. hardly anyone talked to me. it was weird. I felt like the new kid at school or something. but I guess everyone was really tired and everything, plus i was too busy shoving Macho Burritos with green sauce in my mouth. I had never been so hungry in my life. I had two but i felt like I could have had fourteen more.

now, of course, I feel like I could hurl.

the house we're all staying in is really cool. there are at least 10 bedrooms. some of the dancers live here, three of the Men in Black (one of them is actually a woman in black but whatever), and darla. and a guest room for when darcy's dad and kid brother Danny come to visit.

oh yeah and this weird burnout Hawaiian wannabe surfer guy named Walter who runs the kitchen. but he's always in board shorts and surfer tees and he wears pooka shells every day. I think he might be pretty much stoned all the time. I'm definitely going to get to know walter cause he seems like he completely rules.

I'm living on the same floor as darcy and we share a bathroom, which is totally weird. I mean, hi, I'm sharing a bathroom with DARCY BARNES. I'm practically too afraid to go in there.

I keep looking around for Jesse Nixon, that VJ. All day I kept hearing that he was just here or he's coming or whatever. I want to see him already! I wonder if my crush will hold up when I meet him in person? (Notice I said when not if.)

there's a huge living room/kitchen/hangout space down-stairs (they call it The Pit) where everyone chills all the time. it's got a massive flat-screen TV, a big fish tank, and a dartboard with Pashmina's face in the middle. oh and there's a big ol' pool out back with a diving board and there are all these intercoms and stuff all through the house. the basement is all like laundry and stuff. there's a basketball net out front and the yard is all trees and pathways and water features. it's so amazing. I've never even been in a house like this to visit, let alone live. we just don't have it like this down in san diego.

it's all very Real World, very tricked out in every way. I wonder how much it all costs??

I'm exhausted. thank god I get my own room even though it's next door to Darcy's and I can hear Darcy and some guy playing playstation through the wall. at least I think that's what they're doing. they seem to be getting pretty active about it though. my headboard is against that wall and I swear it just moved.

thank god for this laptop.

SlipKnotRules933111: you there?

KellyKelSoCal321: HEY!!!! want to come up this weekend? I have sunday off so maybe we could go to a show on saturday or some-thing. I think cradle of filth might be playing. you can stay in my room.

SlipKnotRules933111: I'll ask mom.

KellyKelSoCal321: don't ask mom. just tell her you're coming. get the bus schedule off the greyhound website. I'll pay you back for the ticket. and BRING MILKY WAYS. lots of them. i'm starving to death. promise??

SlipKnotRules933111: did you watch Cops last night?

D-ZONE, 11:30 PM

Outfit: cotton terry robe darcy gave me. see below.
Hair: it's official, i'm blonder now. I had it done (but not as blond as HER).
Mood: I never knew what tired meant before. not to mention starving to death! darla's a food nazi.
Fortune: Your life is happening now.

---

ok, these people work way harder than I ever imagined. I mean, I watched Popstars. I watched Making the Band. I've seen every Diary and Behind the Music they've ever made. but I had NO IDEA that preparing for a tour was this much work! I thought yesterday was just an especially difficult day, but apparently every day is. here's what we did today:

8 AM—alarm goes off.

8:30 AM—breakfast in the van with the other dancers. all we got was a nonfat yogurt and a piece of fruit because I found out later that someone (I think it was darcy's mom darla) thought we all looked fat yesterday and found out we went to mas macho taco last night so she ordered yogurt and fruit and that's it. maybe I'm fatter than the other dancers. I mean sure some of them are freaks of nature with 0% body fat but I'm not, like, FAT. am I? now I'm paranoid. great.

8:45 AM—van drops us off at gym. weight training. (thank god I got to skip this today. instead I spent the whole time at the gym talking with this Woman in Black who had to put me on the payroll and give me all these forms to send home and everything. good thing I remembered my social security number. I get like $2,000 a week after taxes! I'm LOADED. but I'm not spending it. they're direct depositing it and I'm not taking ANY out. EVER!! I swear.

9:45 AM—van dropped us off at this photo studio where we had to pose in the background for the cover of some magazine Darcy's gonna be on. which means so am I!! so are all the backups. i'm PSYCHED. tito's gonna give me so much crap tho. I thought we were gonna be waiting around all day, sitting there, bored, like they always are on all those Fashion TV behind-the-scenes shows. but we were in and out of there in less than 1 hour. I guess Eileen Wang had called and said that's all darcy could spare. darcy looked amazing even without all that much makeup and stuff on. and her chin zit went away. Was that just last Saturday? Jeez . . .

11 AM—van dropped us off at rehearsal studio (luckily it wasn't that two-way mirror one). an hour of warm-up. a half-hour review of what we did yesterday. everyone's really good. even darcy. I mean yeah she's a little stiff like she can be on tv and stuff but she's so focused and works so hard. it's totally obvious that I'm waaaay behind. but no one's complaining about that or saying anything. at least not to my face. I mean they're not

going out of their way or anything but at least no one's like all over my case. and no, I haven't figured out who's doing who or anything like that. not yet.

12:30 PM—lunch. they brought a tray of turkey cold cuts and skinless chicken breasts into the studio. plus like a ton of cut-up vegetables and some pasta salad. I really wanted southern deep-fried chicken and maybe some ice cream, but hey, whatever. I wasn't gonna complain. oh and Gatorade. I had like three. they gave us 15 minutes to chill out. Today the dancers talked more to one another. everyone else was gossiping about the other tours they'd been on and everything. it seems like everyone knows everyone else on the backup dancer circuit, except me of course. so all I did was stuff my face.

I realized some of the girls were staring at me, watching me eat my second bowl of pasta salad. Which I don't even think is all that much for a full day of dancing. Still, of course my first thought was: They think I'm eating too much. They must think I'm fat. Maybe I am fat? How could I not have noticed? (Channel Tito: Girl, you are not fat. Please.)

1:15 PM—breathing exercises, and the first time since getting here that I really chatted with Darcy. she sat next to me. "Hey K.K.!" for a second I was like "omigod DARCY BARNES is sitting next to me!!" but then I was like, be professional, be professional. stay cool. she told me all about how she's really into yoga ("I just loved that movie where Madonna was a yoga teacher") and how learning how to breathe right can totally make all the difference in fitness and everything. she was like "espe-cially for me, as a singer" and I was like "I sing too!" and she kind of looked at me funny. she goes "but anyway breathing is all about posture and spirituality and stuff. it's so eastern. I love eastern stuff. my friend jesse got me into it. you're going to love it!" and I really wanted to be like "jesse?? what do you mean jesse?? Jesse Nixon? are you going out with him or what??" I mean it's like everyone would want to know that, right? Not just cause I have a crush on him. but i played it cool, being just like "awesome! I'm really into eastern stuff too!" and she was like "i'm coloring my hair later. my hair chick Shaundree's coming over to lighten it. want to do yours too?" I was like "sure!" mostly cause I didn't know what else to say. I was freaking just a little. I noticed two of the other dancers, both guys, looking at me and whis-pering. they turned away when I caught their eyes. had I just done something wrong?

darcy was right, too. the breathing exercises were awe-some. I had so much energy afterward.

2:00 PM—rehearsal. all the chitchat stopped, the flicker of friendliness stopped, and it was down to serious, game-faced business. things started out ok and i've got two numbers down solid already, but I was having a really hard time with this one sequence that ties the two together. there are no breaks in the 2-plus-hour show . . . we're dancing hard the whole entire time. I blew it like four times in a row when Rashid called for a break. we all had powerbars and chilled out for 10 minutes. I'd just closed my eyes for some breathing exercises when I suddenly heard this supershrill woman's voice above me going "K.K.? K.K.?" At first I was like, am I imagining that voice? I was surprised the mirrors weren't cracking. this voice could shatter glass. anyway I opened my eyes and there was darla barnes. WAY scary. she goes: "so, you're K.K., right?" I sat up and was like "yeah" and she goes "I hope you like your new nickname. everyone gets one. Except Darcy of course. I mean, she is the one and only star of the show, so she doesn't need a nickname. everyone knows her name." then darla looked down at my powerbar or whatever it was and goes "is that one of the low-carb ones?" and I go "I don't know" and darla goes "here, give it to me. I'll get you one of the low-carb ones. it's more appropriate for your, um, fitness level." she walked off with my powerbar and never came back. not even with a lo-carb bar.

it's official. they all think I'm fat. So I guess I'm fat.

anyway after that we danced for like another 4½ hours. well everyone else danced for another 2½ hours, then I stayed after with Rashid for some extra help. I have so much to catch up on. I pretty much know about half the show, but I still have to think about every single step. I have to get THERE pretty soon, where it's not my brain that remembers routines, but my legs. speaking of my legs, they are like jello. actually my brain is like jello. I'm a big ol' jiggling bowl of jello.

9:30 PM—Salmon and vegetables. One cup of couscous apiece. SEND EMERGENCY PHISH FOOD NOW.

10:00 PM—darcy grabbed me in mid-bite, halfway through my third stalk of asparagus, squeaking "c'mon! Shaundree is here to do our hair!" I was like "Great!" and we went running up the stairs. (don't worry, I shoved the last of my salmon into my mouth before leaving that table. I wasn't giving up any food for anyone, not even darcy.) anyway we bolted to her bedroom, where there were two temporary beauty parlor chairs set up . . . so we could both get treatments at the same time. darcy spent the whole time flipping through magazines looking for her name and picture. every time she found herself, she'd squeak and show everyone, then complain about the picture ("Lordy I look horrifying don't I?"), then fold down the page and put it on the counter in front of her. if a magazine didn't have any Darcy in it, she'd toss it to me, like her rejects or something. but she was so nice. the whole time she was telling me about how much she misses East Texas, how much she misses her bedroom. Especially her stuffed animal collection. "I have over three thousand Beanie Babies!" I hadn't even heard about beanie babies in forever, and I was thinking are you *kidding me?* then I started thinking maybe she was kidding. so I started to crack up. only, she wasn't laughing. So I blended my laugh into a "that's so awesome!! I only have a couple of beanies!" she goes, "well I can hook you up! I have some duplicates! you can totally have some next time we go home!" before I could say "We?" she goes, "what's your favorite show? mine is Sex and the City! I have all the DVDs! I swear, I AM Carrie Bradshaw. I mean, it's just weird how much alike we are! I wonder if the writers ever use my life as inspiration! Do you think my hair looks better than hers?" luckily right then Shaundree's assistant dunked my head under the water and I couldn't answer or even hear another word.

11:00 PM—my hair is now tiger striped. it's a little freaky. Shaundree says it'll mellow out and look good in a couple of days. anyway Darcy was like good night and we went back to our rooms to crash. except tonight darla knocked on my door like two minutes after I took my top off. I threw on this robe darcy gave me after we got our hair done. (she was all "go take a bath and put this on, then we'll be doing the same exact thing! fun, huh?" I was like, ok cool! but then I cheated and took a shower instead. don't worry I had my hair in a shower cap so I didn't mess up the stripes. ugh.) anyway I let darla in. she was in a tracksuit, sunglasses so dark I couldn't tell where she was looking, and her hair was huge. she was carrying a really big purse and she smelled like peaches. she looks me up and down (at least it looked like she was) and she goes, "hmm. is that one of darcy's robes? you can leave it outside your door tomorrow morning, and i'll make sure it gets washed and returned to darcy's closet." I was like hm. ok. I'm just thinking ok, whatever she wants. this is the boss. I was definitely intimidated. then she goes, "by the way I just wanted to let you know our tour got pushed UP a week. we'll be starting a little early. our first show is June 20 in St. Louis. so we're going to need you in the gym pretty much 24/7 between now and then. I'm afraid that means you'll be working one-on-one with rashid when the other dancers take sunday off. I'm sorry about that. unfortunately that's what happens when dancers show up so many weeks late for rehearsals. But I want you to know just how glad everyone is that you're here. and we're going to need you to pay extra close attention to your, um, fitness. oh by the way we'll just pro-rate your rent and expenses this month and take it out of your pay." it wasn't until then that I realized what was in darla's handbag because it barked. or more like yipped. "Shhh! Punkin!" oh god. she carries a dog in her purse. at least, that's what it sounded like. I couldn't see anything. she kept going, "we'll also deduct your private lessons with rashid. remember, our dancing really matters. if you want to slack off and be sloppy, you should just go dance for Pashmina or some other girl who wants to be as famous as my baby girl but never could be." She left, and I sank onto my bed. So THAT'S who's paying for this whole thing. Me. There's nothing free about this ride. I wonder how much rent is on this place? I know how much private dance lessons are . . . will I have enough to save for evan?

I realized then and there that I would make it a goal to have as little contact with Darla Barnes as possible for the rest of my life.

SlipKnotRules933111: sis
KellyKelSoCal321: hey
SlipKnotRules933111: did u get the tickets?
KellyKelSoCal321: for what

SlipKnotRules933111: I thought you said we were going to see cradle of filth this weekend

KellyKelSoCal321: oh yeah! oh yeah! dude I haven't had time all day. I'm sorry. dude I have bad news I don't get sunday off. they moved the tour date up so I have to do a one-on-one session with Rashid and it starts at 8 am on sunday and i'm so tired already I'm gonna be totally exhausted. I don't know what time I'll even get off on saturday night.

SlipKnotRules933111: so we could see something else. what, don't they have shows like all night in LA?

KellyKelSoCal321: I don't know dude. i haven't been out at all. i'm sorry. I know I said we'd do a show but I don't know. how is it there.

SlipKnotRules933111: carl didn't come home last night and mom's been in her room all day.

KellyKelSoCal321: oh man.

SlipKnotRules933111: so i'm just staying in my room. whatever.

KellyKelSoCal321: what about the twins

SlipKnotRules933111: what about them

KellyKelSoCal321: where are they?

SlipKnotRules933111: I don't know. probably asleep. who cares.

KellyKelSoCal321: oh man. well I guess carl would never think of leaving his precious little blondies alone. lol.

SlipKnotRules933111: this place sucks

KellyKelSoCal321: dude come up on saturday we'll figure something out

SlipKnotRules933111: no it's cool you've got your thing going on I'll be cool

KellyKelSoCal321: HEY!!!! don't be like that!

KellyKelSoCal321: HEY!!!!

KellyKelSoCal321: HEY JACKASS!!

SlipKnotRules933111: downloading . . .

and then he signed off. jerk.

actually, maybe I'm the jerk. I wish I could IM tito, but his parents have grounded him from all web activities other than email since they caught him in an "adult" chat room.

D-ZONE, 12:19 AM

Outfit: official It's Darcy!! concert tee (white on pink), long sleeves
Hair: never blonder
Mood: desperate to CHILL OUT and watch bad tv. need a friend, bad.
Fortune: If you can't say anything nice, keep it to yourself.

---

i've said it before and I'll say it again. thank god for my laptop. I got this email at like 11:20 tonight.

To: kaykay4real
From: Tito_T
Date: Thursday June 5
Time: 11:19 PM
Subject: Daytime hotties
What is going on! I am totally chilling at home watching daytime TV. Port Charles is soooo good! Passions sucks. And I've been totally featuring Regis and Kelly lately. Pretty sad, isn't it. Anyway, enough about me. What is up with you!!! I need to know everything about everyone you've met. Here's what I would like to know: Name, Age, Sign, Hair, Personal Style, Body Type (details if they're hot!), General Description, Why

71

We Care, and Other. OK? Got it? I want
FULL FRONTAL DETAILS. Get it?
Especially DARLA.
Adios,
Moi
PS—And is Darcy dating anyone?

Another one of tito's games. he was probably going to line
up my chart with theirs or something. I love him. ok . . .

To: Tito_T
From: kaykay4real
Date: Thursday June 5
Time: 12:19 AM
Subject: The It's Darcy!! players
ok dude you asked for it you got it. I
don't know everyone's ages or signs. oh
and you can forget appropriate punctuation or any of that crap. sue me.

Name: Darcy Barnes
Age: 18
General Info: She's darcy barnes. What
else do u need to know?
Sign: you already know that she's a Sag.
even though sometimes she gets confused
and says she's an Aries.
Hair: blond. even blonder than me, and
I'm pretty damn blond lately.
Personal Style: believe it or not, off-
stage she's a total jock. I've yet to

see her in anything other than sweats
or workout clothes. although even when
she's in full sweats she somehow manages
to get her belly button exposed, front
and center. so far I've counted four
different belly button rings. I wonder
how many she has to choose from. I bet
she has jewelry designers sending her
belly button rings every day. ps the
weirdest thing in the world is when
she's just standing there listening to
rashid or something, she's always playing with her belly button. you know,
like how some people twirl their hair
or how like evan always has his hand
down his pants when he's watching tv
or whatever, she just fingers her belly
button all the time. ew I said finger.
gross huh.

Body Type: a lot stronger than I expected. kinda like a skier or surfer or
something. muscley legs. abs. she's more
like an athlete than a sexpot. didn't
you tell me once that she did gymnastics
all the time growing up and stuff? are
the boobs real? I don't know for sure.
I'm bad at that stuff. but if they
weren't, would that make getting a nipple pierce less painful? one of these
days maybe I'll ask.

Why We Care: um, she's the star.
Other: I don't know how else to say this but today darcy barnes asked me if I was a virgin. I was like "WHY??" and she was like "because I AM! do you think that's good for my career?" tito you would have GAGGED. so anyway you heard it here first. she claims to be a virgin. and believe it or not, I believe it. (maybe it's her beanie baby collection that's got me believing.) do we even know any other virgins? (I wonder if this factors into her belief that she's so scarily like Carrie Bradshaw . . .)

Name: Darla Barnes
Age: she really wants to be 36, but so does my mom. I'd say she's closing in on 50 fast.
General Info: you probably know more about her than I do, tito. She's darcy's mom and manager and all that. She's always there. But she's not that hip, not like Britney's mom, who seems kind of cool. Darla's more like a beauty-pageant mom.
Sign: I bet she's a scorpio, huh?
Hair: helmet head. think Sally Field in Steel Magnolias. dark hair with tons of products in it, mostly aerosol based. I think she might have had an eye job

because it just seems all too *tight*
around there.

Personal Style: pants suits with cardigans tied across her shoulders. like how
oprah does sometimes. always smells like
peaches. (or is it mangoes?)

Body Type: sort of like Susan Lucci. big
on top with teeny little legs. spends most
of her time sitting down or pacing. (and
lately talking a lot about how untalented
she thinks Pashmina is. ha ha.)

Why We Care: something tells me that
she's the one who's really in charge
around here. and if she's NOT, if I've
got that wrong, then she definitely
WANTS to be in charge. she seems to be
everywhere, all the time, and she seems
to know everyone and everything. she
makes me totally nervous. everyone kisses
up to her all the time. I always suck in
my gut around her because I think she
thinks I'm fat. actually I know she
thinks I'm fat. she practically said so
when she offered everyone else a coke
the other day then handed me a diet
coke. she has this really ugly little
dog that looks like a rat with bows in
its ears and stuff. it slobbers all over
and sounds like it's heaving. she carries it in her purse and talks baby talk

to it and acts like she doesn't notice
when it takes a crap on the floor. it's
called PUNKIN. not "pumpkin" but *PUNKIN*.
Hey, could I make this up?

Other: she acts like it's my fault that
I came late to the tour. sometimes she
gives me this LOOK that makes me feel
like apologizing for being BORN! it's
the kind of look that makes you wish you
could vanish into thin air like in a
star trek movie or whatever. but then
she usually says something like, "thanks
for all your effort" or something totally vice principally like that. know what
I mean? so you're never exactly quite
sure what she means because she never
seems to mean what she says. bizad viz-
ibes. I don't know. i'm just gonna stay
away from her as much as I can.

Name: Eileen Wang
Age: 32, but thinks she's old. I heard
her ordering some anti-aging products
over the phone.
General Info: darcy's tour manager. she
seems constantly in the middle of a crisis. and she talks wicked wicked wicked
superfast. she's from san Francisco and
speaks in mandarin on the phone to her
parents.

Sign: Cancer. she has a crab tattoo on her ankle.

Hair: spiky. pink tips. big square glasses.

Personal Style: I think she's been wearing the same jeans since I met her.

Body Type: boyish. in fact, she turns me on. ha ha ha just kidding.

Why We Care: she DISCOVERED me!! ha ha. :-) and to be honest, I kind of like her. she seems like a regular person, like me.

Other: she spends 99% of her time on the cell phone, usually whispering or panicking. She's always saying stuff like "SHE'S coming!" or "what will SHE think?" SHE, meaning darla. and she (Eileen) seems really scared of her (Darla).

Name: Rashid

Age: 25

General Info: he's the director of the show and he's choreographing the whole thing. he's really focused. and really smart. and he's the only person who ever says anything back to darla. yesterday he disagreed with her about a sequence and he even got his way. she gave him the LOOK and he rolled his eyes. it was too good.

Sign: Sagittarius.

Hair: braids. halfway down his back.

Personal Style: ALWAYS in sunglasses. ALWAYS. (does that mean he's stoned all the time too?)

Body Type: tall, lean, looks incredibly strong, must be a classic ballet dancer or something. posture that almost looks like he's kidding. gorgeous dark skin.

Why We Care: I need all the help I can get. and I gotta say, he's pretty hot. in fact, he's maybe the best eye candy around.

Other: he actually said something nice to me. Unlike anyone else on the tour. He thinks i'm good. he said I've got "it." we were talking about dancing and I told him about what it's like when I dance and I go THERE and he knew exactly what I was talking about. Although now I have to wonder whether or not he's just saying that cause I'm paying him. sigh. whoever said backup dancers live large obviously never got a backup dancer paycheck. I guess it's a good thing I've already had about 350 years of dance training . . . I speak that language, so I'm a quick study. that should cut down on my Rashid bill.

Names: D-Run, Armand, Bart, Li'l D, Jesus, Angeline, the two Tinas, and Waverly.

Ages: 20–30 or so or something

General Info: they're the other backup dancers. they're pretty tight. they're not going out of their way to hang with me or whatever, but they're being pretty patient with me while I play catch-up. I can tell they're watching me tho. trying to figure me out. not that there's anything to figure. I think they're weirded out by the fact that i'm 17. Armand and Jesus are crazy gossips. I think all the guys are gay except for Li'l D, who I think has something going on with one of the Tinas. She sat in his lap all through lunch today, and let's just say that after she got off and Li'l D stood up and readjusted his sweatpants, it was pretty clear that there's nothing Li'l about Li'l D.

Signs: i'll keep you posted.

Hair: around 30–35% real.

Personal Styles: from fringe to frayed jeans to sweats to whatever. Everyone's attached to their iPods. they all have tour jackets like "Nelly 2000" and "Christina: Stripped" and stuff. No one has a Pashmina jacket. I bet Darla banned them.

Body Types: tight, and obsessed with it. these people are constantly stretching, posing, workin' it. I overheard Angeline and Waverly talking about their pilates class and how much it strengthened their core and how much it helped their posture and all that. I should try it cause my posture sucks.

Why We Care: duh they're my backup dancers. ha ha ha!! just kidding. I need to kiss their asses big time. If they don't like me, they could drop me onstage. talk about massive humiliation.

Others: it's a tough clique to break into. but i'm just tryin' to stay cool. they're really good to, uh, eavesdrop on. yesterday they were talking about how Christina Aguilera supposedly has like over 10 piercings. I was like WOW. picture THAT. I mean, WHERE do you put 10 piercings? yikes.

Name: Jesse Nixon

Age: 19

General Info: finally, a superhot VJ. they really got it right this time . . . he's totally cute and totally knows about music. or at least, he's totally good at reading cue cards. anyway I have the kind of crush on him that makes me

feel all giddy like a 9-year-old. Swoon.
Sign: isn't he a leo?
Hair: getting pouffier by the moment.
this is a clear and present problem
Personal Style: you know as well as I do
Body Type: little did I know what
secrets he held until last year's Spring
Fever where he was broadcasting from a
swimming pool and he lifted his shirt
up. can you spell abs?
Why We Care: I haven't laid eyes on him
in person yet but everyone around here
talks about him all the time. Especially
Darla. I don't know if he's even in LA
but it's like every time I turn around
people are talking about him like he
just left the room. and darcy is constantly talking about him—like what he
was wearing on tv or what he said in
some online chat or asking if he's
called. Maybe they're dating, and maybe
they're just friends. I really can't
tell. Like I said, I haven't even seen
him in the flesh yet. Sigh, flesh.
Other: now that I think about it, there's
no way they can be dating. she's a virgin, and he's too hot to wait around for
her. that is, if she's really a virgin.

D-ZONE, JUST WAKING UP

Mood: confused. when I woke up this morning I thought
I was in my bed at home.
Outfit: piggly wiggly pjs
Fortune: Believe the hype.

To: kaykay4real
From: Tito_T
Date: Friday June 7
Time: 8:14 AM
Subject: Re: The It's Darcy!! players
Thanks for the rundown. Sounds like quite
a crew. No one you can't deal with.
No, we don't know any virgins. Including
Darcy Barnes. I don't care if she has a
trillion Beanie Babies. And another clue to
catch: She's *definitely* dating Jesse Nixon.
I can tell! Just today there was a gossip
item online about how they were together
at a Dodgers game and his hand was on her
knee the whole time. Is it true?
Stay away from Rashid. Sounds like someone's got a crush. I can tell that one's
gonna be trouble.
PS—Have you seen Darcy's website? Google
her and see for yourself.
Tito

I knew about Darcy's site. It's this pink and baby blue website where Darla keeps a diary about Darcy. crazy, huh? what she does, where she goes, supposedly like some kind of "behind the scenes" about what really happens backstage. god if I'm ever famous I hope my mother doesn't act like an idiot.

May 30, 2003

Darcy's such a neat freak! She always has been. I think she gets it from me! I know I never have to worry about her keeping her room clean and her clothes ironed. And speaking of her clothes, people say she dresses sexy, but I think she just looks beautiful. My baby just takes my breath away!!

I was like yeah right. She has a staff who does her ironing. Then I read this one.

June 1, 2003

Darcy just informed me today that she has a HUGE crush on one of her backup dancers. I can't tell you which one because I don't want it to get out, but . . . she's been hinting that she wants to ask him out! I said he's just too old for her, but if I know Darcy, she'll find a way to sneak in a date behind my back! That girl! I just hope the press doesn't get ahold of this info! ;-)

The important thing is that I know I can
trust her to make truly adult decisions
no matter what. She'll never go too far
with a boy, and she'll never let a boy
get in the way of her career. Besides if
she messes up she knows she'll have to
deal with her mama!!

What? Darcy's hot for a dancer? I wonder if it's rashid
she's after? oh, great. damn! no way! there goes my
master plan to ensnare his heart and begin a lifetime
together making music and children. and swimming
laps in our pool. ok wait, maybe tito's right. maybe she
IS dating jesse and this is just a big hoax. maybe darla's
just saying this.

Ugh.

does this mean I have to cancel my crush?

D-ZONE, 11 PM

Outfit: Rashid lent me his Etnies hoodie. it's HUGE.
Hair: sweaty.
Mood: Alone at last. I finally feel like an official member of this tour. I think it feels pretty good but I'm not 100% sure.

"So, how does it feel to be my new best friend?"

Darcy Barnes said that to me last night. I know, weird, huh? ok lemme back up.

I have spent the last 24 hours straight with darcy barnes. nonstop. she needs Ritalin.

I saw a different side of her. or more like a few different sides of her. I mean, she doesn't really seem like what you think darcy barnes would be like. not like her pictures and videos and interviews and stuff. I mean, I knew she wasn't going to be *exactly* like that or anything, but . . . I don't know . . . I guess I just expected someone cooler. someone edgier. someone a little bit hipper than me. don't get me wrong, she's nice and everything, but there's something weird about her . . . it's like she just hasn't really gotten that far around the block. she goes from acting like a grownup to acting like a little kid without any kind of notice. like one minute she's arguing with Eileen about who her "demographic" is like a total Man in Black, and the next minute she's on the phone to darla, all "mom can you come to brush my hair the way I like it?" like she's 7. it's weird. but I'll admit she's kind of charming. so far.

but I guess she doesn't really have any friends her own age or anything so I guess it's normal to be weird. (how funny: "Normal to be Weird" . . . that should be the name of her biographical tv movie of the week.) anyway, she has no friends, so maybe that's why she's been totally glommed onto me for the last day and night. or maybe it's just because jesse (her "friend"/boyfriend, still not sure) isn't around. or maybe she does this to everyone she meets. well whatever. even if I'm suspicious about it I've been having a good time hanging out with her. we actually get along!

ok wait I said I was gonna back up didn't I. ok. yeah. after basically hardly seeing her since getting here (except from behind, in rehearsals), darcy dove headfirst into my personal space last night and only now just left.

she came to my room at like midnight. I was in bed with the lights out. she didn't even knock, she just came right on in, threw on the lights (all of them. which, if I can just say so, is way, *way* too many), and bounced over into my bed. not just onto my bed, but actually into it. like she bounced up and slid under the covers in one smooth move. I was kinda like um, after age 12, you're not allowed to just get in bed with me unless you *really* know me. but I didn't say it out loud. I'm just glad I was wearing my pj bottoms.

anyway she was waving this random newsletter thing, Pop Star Tour Report Weekly or something, which I'd never heard of before. she goes "K.K.! Check it out! You're famous!" and sure enough, there I was.

MOVERS AND SHAKERS

Hollywood Hustle Wire Service, Los Angeles—The It's Darcy!! tour announced today that K.K. Kimball will replace Shania Johnson in the Darcy Barnes "It's Darcy!!" lineup. Eileen Wang, tour manager, explained how she found this newcomer, rumored to also be in the running for the coveted "lead dancer" spot: "We wanted a fresh face, someone with no dance experience whatsoever. We found her in a San Diego teen nightclub. Even though she's never had a dance lesson, her raw talent and energy are a great addition to the company." Darcy Barnes commented, "It's great! Me and K.K. are totally like best friends now! We do everything together!"

that's where the "how's it feel to be my new best friend" part comes in.

I didn't answer. I didn't know what to say. I mean I don't feel like her best friend. how could we be best friends? we'd barely met!

but when someone tells you that you're their best friend, you can't say sorry, nice try, but you're not. Especially when it's your EMPLOYER . . . not to mention the biggest pop star in the universe! I looked around to see if there were cameras on us, like this was Punk'd or something . . .

but I realized she was kind of serious. I mean like I said, it's not like she has any friends her own age.

besides, maybe to her a "best friend" is just another person on the payroll. like, manager, agent, publicist, stylist, best friend . . . hey, I'm not going to argue, this could be fun. let's just be clear that it's K.K. who's the best friend. not Kelly. Kelly's best friend is and always will be the one and only, the lovely, the fabulous, the sorely-missed-especially-right-now Tito.

At that point it kind of sank in that they'd made up this whole story about me not having any dance training, which got under my skin, big time, because as previously stated I've had 350 years of training. but I didn't really have a chance to dwell on it too much.

so i just squealed and hugged her. you know, kind of like how people greet each other at the airport. for some reason it just seemed like the thing to do at the time. it was K.K.'s squeal, not Kelly's.

darcy was like so what should we do first, best friend? now that we do everything together?

I was like I don't know. and then she goes, "is there anything good on tv?" and grabs my remote and starts flipping around. she picks up the phone and goes, "walter? WALTER? can you bring us some corn nuts and diet dr. pepper? CORN NUTS!! no, not barbecue. plain. the big bag. yeah. also some chicken. do you have any fried chicken? you do? I knew it. you rule. ok, I'm in shania's old room. no, shania's not here anymore. the new girl is

K.K. yeah K.K. she's my best friend now, didn't you hear? her name is K.K. . . . . K.K.! ok. bye." I was thinking, Corn nuts? Gross, then I noticed my stomach growling and realized they actually sounded delicious. I mean Darla's little diet is making me crazy for food. any food.

anyway then Darcy looks at me and goes, "it's cool if I hang out in here tonight, right? I'm so bored with my room and I haven't talked to Jess—" she cut herself off before she finished the thought, which was a little frustrating. I mean if I'm going to be her best friend, shouldn't I know whether she and jesse are "just friends" or more?

then she started flipping the channels again. MTV was doing a special on her. "Oh Lordy, they're using that footage from when I was Female Hottie of the Millennium at the Teenz Rule Awards! Ew! do you think my hair looks better than Jessica Simpson's? Do you think she ever wears a wig? Do you think I should?" then she started flipping again and didn't stop until she hit The Wizard of Oz, which was on some random family cinema cable channel. it was that first scene in munchkinland and she's bursting into "We REPRESENT the Lollipop Guild! The Lollipop Guild!" and she's like don't you LOVE the munchkins?

my inner kelly wanted to be like, no, actually, they scare me and I had nightmares about 'em when I was a child. oh and also I was asleep before you came in here. but K.K. was like yeah they're so cute! I even squealed a little.

she goes "That's where I got the inspiration for 'Love You Like a Lollipop!'" I was just thinking something tells me that connection is probably lost on most people when they hear your song, but ok!

then I was like wait. can this be? can the biggest pop star in the world, the Female Hottie of the Millennium, role model to girls everywhere, wet dream to boys everywhere . . . can darcy barnes really be this boring and dopey? where's the booze? where are the boys gone wild? where's the girl I know so well from "celebrities uncensored" not to mention "behind the music"? where are the true Hollywood story moments already?

a minute later a commercial came on and I just blurted, hey, about this clipping. how come Eileen made me seem like such an untrained dancer? I took like 350 years of lessons, I mean 12 years, I mean I don't care but it's a little strange. Darcy didn't know what I was talking about so I read the clipping out to her. I was like Eileen knows what my real story is. how come she made this one up?

"Oh, that," said Darcy. "We just thought it would be a good angle. everyone has a story, you know? I mean, it's not that big of deal, it's not like anyone's really going to check up on you or anything. I mean, it's better for everyone if we figure out what story we want and sort of stick you into it. so we had this big meeting last night about you and eileen said that this story makes you seem more real than your other story." Funny that she called my real story my "other story." she finished up with "believe me this is better for your career, too."

I was pretty weirded out that there was a roomful of people making up my background without my even knowing about the meeting so I kind of just clamped my mouth shut. maybe she's right. it feels weird but what do I know. she HAS been in the business for, like, half her life. besides, it's not like I'm going to quit right now. this is too good of a gig. I hope she's right. I hope no one I know sees it.

and she goes, "but don't you love the best friend part?" I gave up right then and there. I squealed and hugged her again. besides, I reminded myself, I wasn't Kelly anyway. I was k.k., darcy barnes's best friend. at least that's who I'd be for the next couple months.

then she goes "do you have a boyfriend?" and I go no. she looked at me for a minute and I got kinda nervous so I said, "we just broke up last week," which I totally made up just to fill the space and besides, maybe this fictional K.K. really did have an ex. hey, I could get into this fake-me thing . . . anyway so darcy made this sad face and I said, "no it's no big deal. forget about him. he's a loser and you're here now. forget him," and she smiled. I could tell the conversation wasn't over. so I said, "do YOU have a boyfriend?"

and she said, "yeah." so I said omigod, is it Rashid?

she goes, huh?

I go, you know. that's what it said on your website.

darcy goes, oh lordy NO, that's my crazy mother making

stuff up. I was like why would she do that and darcy was like um, well, I guess it's good for my image to have a crush on him and he is kind of hot, I mean, I totally love him but I barely know him . . . he just sort of works for me, you know?

I was thinking yeah! he's fair game!

then I was like ok well who IS it? someone from home or something? and she goes no not really. then she smiled and said she doesn't want to talk about it because she misses him. she misses all her friends from home. she was like I lost most of my friends when I became Darcy Barnes but they're a bunch of jealous people and I don't want to talk about it.

so I shut up. I mean, it was like she ripped open her brain for me there for a second but didn't really let herself finish her thoughts. I guess we have all summer. I mean, I'm not about to get all up in her face about it even though i kept thinking how Tito will KILL me if i don't find out. give it time, I figured.

then I was like omigod, she lost all her friends when she became Darcy Barnes. does that mean I'm going to lose mine now that I've become K.K.? Too late.

then she goes, You know I'm a virgin right?

I go, are you really? I mean, I've heard it but I didn't know.

she goes, do you think I'm lying? I go, no I mean I just know that the papers make stuff up sometimes right? like that thing about you and jesse and all that.

she goes, *"THAT'S NOT TRUE!"*

and I go, I know! that's what I'm saying, they make stuff up! but of course I was thinking damn that really got her revved up. it must be true. i wonder . . .

and she goes, well I am. I am a virgin.

and I go, Um, ok!

and she goes, I just want people to know that.

and I was just like, "I totally understand" even though I totally didn't. why do people need to know that? why do I need to know that?

then she goes, are you a virgin? not that there's anything wrong with not being one it's just . . . are you?

and I was like what kind of question is that? I rolled my eyes and laughed. "I'm so sure!" I said. I figured that was about as noncommittal as I could get without full-on lying.

then she goes, "Can you keep a secret?" and I said yeah and she said, "don't tell my mom," and she pulled down the waistband of her jockey for hers (I was like WHAT'S GOING ON) then showed me a teensy weensy tattoo of a dolphin. "mama said I can do whatever I want in the whole world . . . except get a tattoo. ha! don't tell her. no one knows. I got it in brazil when I was there with . . ." and before she said who she was with she goes, "oh, sorry. can't say. I promised. that whole boyfriend thing. uh, I mean crush thing. oh, whatever. anyway isn't it the CUTEST tattoo?"

she goes, "wanna go get a tan? I have side-by-side tan-ning beds in my gym downstairs and I know where eileen hides her vodka!"

Bingo! Behind-the-music moment! Here we go . . .

K.K., backup dancer and party girl said, "um, SURE! Totally!!" even while Kelly, exhausted dancer, was think-ing, hey what about the CORN NUTS?!

we finally got to sleep (me with a slight midnight tan-ning bed sunburn and darcy with slightly slurred words) at like 3 AM. darcy slept in my bed (which would be a true Hollywood story moment except that it was more like a sweet valley twins moment).

the last thing she said before drifting off was, "G'night, best friend. Hey, I wonder who Pashmina's best friend is these days? she's probably some loser."

I lay there for a while trying to figure out what she meant. No luck. the best I could do was just decide that darcy was, in fact, an alien from outer space. The longer I thought about it in the dark by myself, the funnier it seemed. I actually giggled myself to sleep.

how psycho is that?

D-ZONE, LUNCH BREAK, 12 PM

Outfit: I'm singin the capezio blues?
Hair: stringy, sweaty, dirty . . . but blond.
Mood: The grind

I woke up to darcy barnes howling at the top of her lungs in the room next to mine.

Aaaaaaiiiiiiiiiiiiiiii! Aaaaaaaaaaaaiiiiiiiiiiiiiii!

of course my first thought was dang if she's a virgin I'd like to know exactly what's going on in there . . .

but then I realized she was really screaming. there must have been something really really wrong. was she being attacked? where were the men in black?

I sprang out of bed, raced to the hallway, sprinted down to her door. there was a woman in black standing out-side. I screamed, Can't you hear? she's in there scream-ing! I dove over the woman in black and lunged for the doorknob. I burst in, and there was darcy, standing there topless, looking in the full-length mirror and screaming like a crazy person. I was like ARE YOU OK???

and she just went quiet and turned around. hey K.K., she whispered. I'm fine! I'm just warming up my voice. I have a recording session in a couple of hours, and I like it better when it's kind of scratchy. Don't you?

yup, alien from outer space. that sounds just about right.

since then we've been dancing pretty much nonstop. I am SORE. I'm SERIOUS. so this is how the dancers get their bodies so tight. dancing their asses off every day, all day. luckily it seems like I'm getting fewer looks from Armand and Jesus. And Li'l D and his Tina are starting to be way more, uh, open. Make that public. in fact, I'm pretty sure their public displays of affection could get them arrested in some states.

But the good news is I finally got THERE this morning, during my private session with Rashid. he's been helping me out with this one transition that's been driving me crazy. it involves a spin that I have to enter fast, then slow down in the middle, then come out of fast again. it's not easy, and being three weeks behind and the only one in the crew who doesn't have it down yet makes it even harder. and the more I kept trying and failing, the more my confidence got sapped. so I asked him if he had time. he said yes, he had a half-hour. he's the best.

it was actually more like an hour and a half but by the end, I totally had it down. Rashid goes "kel" (he calls me "kel," which is way better than K.K. if you ask me . . . it makes me really listen to him), "what I need is for you to do it like you just did on every dance, every night. you need to get there every single time. do you have that in you?"

I didn't answer. I didn't know the answer. rashid told me to think about it, then he left.

SlipKnotRules933111: I can't come tonight. I don't have enough for a bus ticket.

KellyKelSoCal321: dude it's $16

SlipKnotRules933111: I know

KellyKelSoCal321: I think u can scrounge it.

SlipKnotRules933111: i tried.

KellyKelSoCal321: go in my room and get my secret $20. it's under the lamp next to my bed.

SlipKnotRules933111: don't you know? the village of the damned twins moved into your room

KellyKelSoCal321: are you KIDDING me? are you SERIOUS? I cannot BELIEVE that.

SlipKnotRules933111: so your twenty probably isn't there anymore

KellyKelSoCal321: damn! well how much do you have.

SlipKnotRules933111: $11.

KellyKelSoCal321: ask Mom you dink.

SlipKnotRules933111: she wouldn't even let me go if she knew, let alone pay for it. I have to sneak out as it is. what am I going to do?

KellyKelSoCal321: I'll get tito to meet you at the bus station tomorrow. I can't believe it's this hard to scrounge money for a bus ticket. it's so jerry springer. what time is the bus?

SlipKnotRules933111: 4:30

KellyKelSoCal321: ok I'll tell tito. be there on time.

D-ZONE, OMIGOD IT'S 3:15 AM

Outfit: Darcy's acid-wash jeans. they are so 80s I love them.
Mood: Kinda wiped out in that awesome way when you're having so much fun.
Fortune: You're young now. You won't be later.

---

saturday was like the hardest day yet of dancing. we got done at like 7, and I went straight to my room, where I knew I had a half-hour to rest before I had to go pick up evan. it felt like I had barely put my head down when my pager went off.

DUDE WHERE R U

it was from Evan. omigod I forgot! he was at the bus station. it was 11 PM. he'd been there for three, no four hours! that is, if he was still there. I went to throw on some clothes and splash water on my face, hoping to bolt out of there with no one noticing.

and ran into darcy in the bathroom. she looked like she'd been crying. her eyes were all red and she was kind of short of breath and her hair was a disaster. "what are you doing?" she asked. I told her. she immediately perked up, going, "no WAY!! lemme drive you! I just got a new Navigator yesterday! we'll sneak out and go!" I said, "dude no way aren't you exhausted?" and she said, "no way let me just grab a baseball cap" and I go, "what's wrong? you look like you've been crying" and she goes, "nothing. nothing big. just jesse. he was supposed to come this weekend but now he's not. it totally bums me out when he blows me off like that. I keep thinking he'll change."

I was like but I thought you were just friends!

she paused for a minute, inhaled deeply like she was going to say something, but stopped short. "we are. he's just a friend. a really annoying friend" all sad, then she goes, "but whatever, let's get out of here. I'd love to get out for a drive."

I was like well, well, well. the plot thickens. I'm still not convinced they're going out. I mean they talk on the phone like three times a day and darcy's always talking about him. but she's sticking to the "friend" story. Though sometimes it's "best friend" and today it's "really annoying friend."

but sorry, tito, I'm not about to get a smackdown for asking too many questions. I mean, I'm sure I'll find out soon enough.

also, I wonder if Jesse's a total jerk after all. Could my celebrity crush possibly be a jerk?

so we headed out. doesn't seem like a big deal for a megafamous pop star and a high school girl of driving age but we had to sneak out because all those men in black don't like it when darcy takes off alone and if darla ever found out I can only imagine how pissed she would get. she'd probably withhold food from the entire company for a whole day. darcy pretends to be like "whatever" about her entourage, but I can tell she likes it. plus I did hear she had some stalker in texas who offered her big $$ for her virginity . . . hello, stalker! anyway we made it to the garage and out onto the street without being noticed.

if there's one thing I've learned in the last week or whatever it's that I have no clue. these people are so strange. I mean darcy the alien's got at least three personalities so far:

1. the superhard worker

2. the little kid watching Disney flicks

3. the heartbroken girlfriend

and now there appeared to be a fourth: a seize-the-day, crazy, let's sneak out and misbehave chick. this one was my favorite.

the other thing is, sometimes it seems like she's in charge, running the whole show, and sometimes it seems like a whole elaborate show set up by darla and eileen and all those people in black without darcy having anything to do with it. I don't know. the only thing I can say with certainty is that darcy barnes has no business having a driver's license. that girl is danger behind the wheel. we're talking Thelma-like driving. or was it Louise?

at the first stoplight she actually obeyed (which was

about four stoplights from our start point), she turned to me and said, This is fun. Thanks for letting me come. I never get to do anything fun with anyone I actually like. this whole best friend thing isn't that bad, is it? then she turned up the radio and started jamming out to the white stripes. Another surprise—I didn't think she listened to real rock.

when we got to the bus station I'd almost forgotten where we were going. but there was evan, all by himself, sitting outside the entrance on his knapsack, with his headphones on, bobbing his head and smoking a cigarette.

we drove up and I hung out of the Navigator screaming EVAN PUT THAT SHIT OUT! he isn't a smoker, he just does it sometimes to look tough. he's so 9th grade.

anyway, he wasn't that mad about us being late. he said it was pretty cool hanging out at the bus station. but evan's like that. he likes wandering around alone checking people out and "looking tough." I think it makes him feel really independent or something. he wasn't even all that upset that we missed a show. I think he was just so glad to be away from home, on his own, even if it was so far mostly at the bus station, even if it was only for a few hours.

oh, and when I introduced him to darcy he goes, "what's your name again?" he totally didn't recognize her. ha! she laughed at him. "you don't know?" he goes, "sorry, I forgot . . . my bad." and she goes, "that's AWESOME! I love you!"

I wondered when the last time was that darcy met someone who didn't already know who she was, someone who didn't already have ideas and expectations about who she should be. Probably like never. She seemed almost thankful.

you know how I was just saying how I needed a friend? tonight, I was almost starting to feel like I had one.

anyway the three of us decided to just cruise around Santa Monica in the Navigator listening to the radio. evan kept flipping the station around like a maniac. even when there was a song he was into, he'd still hit "scan." he's such a boy. but every time one of darcy's songs came on (and three of them did: "Love You Like a Lollipop," "Whenever," and "Kooky") she would insist we turn it up full blast, roll down the windows, and sing at the top of our lungs. evan didn't know any of the words but he tried.

Darcy and evan talked a LOT about pyrotechnics and fires. Darcy's really into that stuff too. they talked about it, seriously, on and off the whole night. I guess pyromaniacs have a lot to say to each other. I was thinking how weird it is that they probably both have it in 'em to burn down a building, only evan actually did it. I wonder if that means they both have it in 'em to be pop stars, too. then I wondered if I had it in me. anyway she kept saying how she always wanted tons of explosions and stuff in her show. the whole thing kinda freaked me out a little given evan's deal with burning down the organic grocery but whatever.

it was kind of cute that he and darcy got along so well. it was nice to see her being so cool with him. I mean, I'm the first to admit that it's not easy to get along with my brother, but darcy and he were like long lost buds.

I was digging this new darcy. I wondered how often it came out and if it ever existed in the D-Zone.

darcy kept asking evan if he would ever cheat on a girlfriend. he kept being like, HUH? But she just kept asking. finally he figured out that he should say "No," though, and started saying that instead. so Darcy goes, "see, there are good men out there. don't ever become a vj, evan." he just laughed. luckily he was having too much fun to pay attention too closely.

Evan goes, Where are you from anyway? to Darcy and she goes, Texas! and she goes, "Dang I wish we were back in Texas so we could go cow tipping!" then she goes, "Evan, can I have a cigarette?"

he goes, yeah but I got a joint too.

I was like WHAT?? evan what the HELL? isn't that a probation violation? gimme that! what the hell are you doing?

and darcy was like "omigod you have pot??"

she pulled into the 7-11 parking lot and was like come on let's smoke it.

I was like I cannot smoke pot with my brother! and Darcy goes oh relax. no one's going to find us. do you

103

think I'd risk my reputation? it's no big deal. And I was like well, maybe not for you, but he's MY brother. and she goes, evan hand me that joint and your lighter.

Sometimes you just gotta go with it. rock on, girl.

it was the most fun I've had since I got here. evan forgot the Milky Ways I'd asked him to bring but darcy gave him $40 and he went into the 7-11 and got nachos, sour patch kids, combos, and slurpees. we pigged out! screw darla.

did I mention that darcy is an INSANE driver?

D-ZONE, LUNCH

Outfit: all business: tracksuit and headband.
Mood: A little manic. The show debuts in less than TWO WEEKS.
Fortune: Free lunch? Are you kidding?

---

darla decided to give us all an early start today as in 8 AM on a sunday. you know, the morning after last night, which had only ended a couple of hours before. I wonder if she did it on purpose because deep down she knew that I'd been out with her darling daughter, inhaling illegal drugs and running stoplights and potentially jeopardizing her entire public image.

Bleary-eyed and bitchy, I desperately chowed a banana and sucked down two big iced coffees (nonfat milk, no sugar, ICK). that's all we got to eat. that's all walter put out for us. he looked at me like "sorry" and looked over at darla. "master's orders" he mouthed. yup, she knew. sigh. and this was exactly the kind of morning I could have used an egg mcmuffin, know what I mean?

I guess we were being punished for having any fun last night and I heard darla and darcy arguing in low voices in the hall about how much gas is in the Navigator's tank. they were like whisper-yelling, like they're always doing on soaps. "But it's MY car mama!"

"It's OUR car baby. But you need your sleep!"

"Yeah so I can make more money for you?!"

"Is that how you talk to your mama?"

this is nothing like their public relationship. I mean, the two of them act like best buds on camera. if only people could hear the way they scream at each other in person. I even heard the word "bitch," twice. But I just kept my eyes on my banana.

evan was staying in my room, and I just let him keep sleeping. I figured I'd probably be back before he got up anyway. I told him to sleep or watch tv and not to come out. I just hoped darla wouldn't wander in there and find him. I could just picture her now. she'd probably accuse me of having underage boys up to my room. not that there's any rule or anything about having guests, and I do pay rent don't I? anyway I just don't really need to be messing with darla at ALL. especially today when I can barely see straight.

I went over to darcy and smiled at her. I go, How are you? are you ok?

and she goes, Yeah why wouldn't I be ok?

and I go, But after last night?

and she just goes, Of course I'm ok! are YOU ok? are you ready to dance? we need 110% today.

and I go, but what about jesse?

and she looked at me with cross-eyes and goes, "what do

you mean? you mean Jesse Nixon? whatever, who cares."

part of me was like ok, sorry for asking. damn! I guess we were back to Diva Darcy, we left Cool Chick Darcy way behind. but she wasn't being mean or anything. she just seemed incredibly focused.

anyway we danced all morning, hard, until 12:30. I've never sweated so much in my life. I think Darla told Rashid to drill us extra hard. that wasn't unusual all by itself, but there was definitely something different going on today.

all of a sudden, everyone seems really anxious about how soon the tour is. everyone's all "ten days till St. Louis ten days till St. Louis! that's where the tour starts off. anyway I have a feeling that things aren't going to be as loose as last night from now on. there's a sense of dread in the air.

anyway after this morning's session, which I don't mind saying totally sucked, I raced back to D-Zone, woke up evan, and gave him $15 for cab fare back to the bus station. oh and $16 for the bus.

Then I gave him another fifty bucks. what can I say, my first check was deposited on friday. (instead of $2,000 it was more like $400, what with all the "rent" and "private lessons" and "management fees" they took straight out of my check but whatever.) I told him to behave.

quit acting like my mother, he said.

I was like, Someone needs to act like your mother, Evan. I know you're not getting it at home. he laughed.

I loaded him into his taxi, waved goodbye, and headed back to the studio. I've still got an hour to work on that transition before we start group rehearsals again.

D-ZONE, LATE

Outfit: I ♥ Darcy Barnes tee. I cut the sleeves off.
Mood: Pumped.
Fortune: Bite your tongue and remember.

To: Tito_T
From: kaykay4real
Date: Monday June 10
Time: 10:15 PM
Subject: getting THERE
I finally met Jesse Nixon today. where
do I start? for starters he's as cute as
he looks on TV and stuff. And taller
than I thought . . . he's a good package
overall. He needs to cool it with the
trucker hats but whatever.
Anyway, he's a total player. He was in
the pit with darcy and I was the only
one there, watching tv on the couch.
darcy was like that's k.k. she's the new
girl in the crew. he totally came up and
sat right next to me, I mean RIGHT next
to me . . . started rapping. "New girl!
New girl! When you gonna do me girl?" I
was like ew but I didn't want to cause a
scene so I just laughed and squirmed
away. He squirmed after me. I was officially grossed out. Darcy goes "leave

her alone!" and they left. It was gross.
Dude we are working so hard. I'm so
sorry I haven't written. I totally
haven't been able to even concentrate
hardly at all. Thanks for lending Evan
that money last week. Did he pay you
back yet? I gave him some $$. If he didn't,
let me know so I can kick his ass.
We've been dancing like 12 hours a day.
For the first few days, I was just so
tired at the end of the day that I
thought I would just totally pass out. But
now that I'm really starting to get the
routines down, I'm getting better. my abs
are seriously tight right now! and darla
hasn't commented on my weight in days.
anyway, darcy continues her totally
schizo behavior . . . but added all up,
I think I like her pretty well. and
don't believe everything you read about
"best friends." You are my one and only,
tito. forever and ever.
Anyway I'm starting to get pretty
freaked out about the show. it's coming
up in nine days. I have nine days to get
perfect. and the thing is, I still
haven't really bonded with the dancers.
I still get looks from them like I'm
some kind of amateur. I guess it's
because I'm younger than them but I

can't help feeling they're annoyed that
I'm friends with darcy or something.
what do you think? it's not like they
want me to fail, but they don't want me
to be too good or something. I don't
know. I don't get it, I thought we were
supposed to work together.
Why aren't you here with me?
L8er,
Kelly aka K.K.
PS—Punkin the Pekinese is seriously annoying.

The rest of the day sucked completely. I mean, it
started out well enough. I felt like I was starting to go
THERE in a couple of places.

rashid even asked me to be, like, darcy's stand-in on a
few of the numbers since she wasn't there. (maybe she
had a photo shoot or went off with jesse, who knows?)
the guys (armand and jesus) used me to practice the lift
that they normally do with darcy.

as a crew we really nailed some stuff. when we came to
the end of "Indentured to Me," I was like hang on guys
I have to take a whiz. I bolted for the bathroom because
I seriously needed to pee! they laughed behind me. for
the first time it sounded like they were laughing with
me instead of at me.

but just as I was about to shut the door behind me
someone blocked it open. I knew it was darla even
before I saw her—I smelled peaches.

I peeked around and looked up at her. her lipstick was fresh, her hair was perfect, and even through her wrap-around sunglasses I could tell she had the LOOK on.

"you looked really good out there today K.K.," she goes. "you seem to be picking up on the moves right." I mumbled thanks and tried to walk past her into the bathroom. "it's a good thing you've learned the stuff because we open next week."

and again I started mumbling, this time about how psyched I was and how much work I know we need to do but we'll get there. and then she goes, "that's nice to hear that you're dedicated. But K.K. let me be very clear"—and she actually put her hand on my shoulder all faking like she was being sensitive or caring or some-thing—"rashid seems to think you're very talented. and you seem to have no problem doing anyone's steps, including darcy's. but let's all remember why we're here. we're here because of darcy. she is the star and the reason we have jobs. and do you know why darcy is here? darcy is here because of me. and no matter what was running through your mind during today's rehearsals, no matter what rashid or any of the others asked you to do, it's entirely inappropriate for you to sub in for darcy's steps, even in rehearsal. you are NOT the star here, do you understand? darcy has enough competi-tion from pashmina, britney, and all the rest. don't even THINK that you'll ever be added to that list."

she stepped closer. I was totally cornered and near panic.

I just looked at her as blankly as I could even though I was terrified on the inside. "I know all of you teen girls have dreams of making it big. maybe they even told you back in, where was it, santa cruz? santa barbara? wherever, maybe they even told you that you had what it takes to make it big. everyone says things like that to make girls like you, regular girls with regular hair and regular bodies, feel better."

"actually come to think of it, it was probably good for them to have to lift you today. next to lifting you, lifting darcy will be a breeze for them."

OUCH, I thought. this is only going to get worse. I stared at the floor, unable to stop blinking.

"but I digress. you see, K.K., stardom doesn't happen for girls like you, ever. it only happens for girls like darcy, girls who are not regular. girls who are special. you, K.K., are a support player. backup. your only purpose here is to make darcy look good. that means getting the moves down and not screwing up. it does NOT mean standing out. after all, we can't all be darcy barnes, now, can we? it would be silly to spend your whole life dreaming about being a star. because for you, that's impossible. have I made myself clear?"

I just stared at her mouth. I started blinking really fast so I wouldn't cry. I refused to let her make me cry. she actually reached out to grab my chin and pull my face up but I jerked away. "let me say again, J.J., I mean K.K., that we're all just thrilled to have you here."

thanks I mumbled. just then that Pekinese stuck its head up out of her purse and sneezed. I'm sorry, I like animals and all, but ick.

I wanted to bop it on the head. I didn't. I just concentrated on breathing, slowly, deeply, carefully.

Darla went on. "and just so you know, I won't be telling darcy about this little chat or the incident this afternoon . . ." again with the mumbling: thanks. and then she goes, "remember, I'll be watching from behind the glass, cheering you guys on throughout all your rehearsals." with that she turned and left. I closed the door of the bathroom, turned to the mirror, and stared at myself for about an eighth of a second before bursting into big sloppy gaspy blubbery snotty really wet sobs.

I cried for a while before I realized that for all I knew darla was watching me from behind THAT mirror too.

I wanted out, out of everything. but only for a minute. when I thought about evan, when I thought about the money, I changed my mind. I need to nail this gig. I want every penny owed to me. this could be evan's ticket out. not to mention my own.

D-ZONE, 11 PM

Rashid just left. he came up to my room a little while ago to see how I was doing. I guess it was pretty obvious that I was upset after I came back out of the bathroom. maybe it was the fact that I was beet red . . . not just my skin but my eyes and he totally figured out why.

at first when he knocked I was kind of thinking, um, leave me alone you totally ruined my day by having me sub in for darcy when you knew that darla was watching. but then I decided to let him in because it wasn't fair to blame him. we were just practicing, right? I'd even forgotten that darla would be watching.

he said to me, "look, it's cool. darla can be tough. I know I put you in a rough spot. I apologize, and believe me I won't do that again. but you're really good, girl. you've got IT, like I said. I saw in your face today that you, what do you call it, got THERE while you were dancing. you are the real thing, Kel." I love it when he calls me that. No one else on the tour ever does. He's the only person who sees me.

Then he told me that sometimes I need to keep my realness to myself. sometimes it makes the other dancers feel threatened or something. he said that he knows the hardest thing for me isn't going to be the dancing. it's going to be learning how to deal with

everything else. like being treated roughly by the people in charge and having to put up with second-class
treatment and having to practically beg for raises and
having to stay on your toes with everyone else 24/7. but
he says he thinks they're chilling out and who knows
maybe I'll make friends.

"you're a good enough dancer to do this, kel. it's just
your skin that needs to get thicker."

ok so he sounds like a camp counselor but actually,
that's exactly what I need right now.

his cellie rang. it was eileen. she said she wanted to talk
to me. I go, hello?

"hey there k.k. how are you wow you guys looked so
good today this is going to be the best tour ever and
rashid told me he's really really happy with all your work
and everything and I'm just really psyched but I guess I
should have really been more clear about what darla
expects from everyone and well I just want you to know
that she's really got her eye on you I mean I think it's
just because she really really likes you and she's really
really counting on you and everything but I know sometimes that can be a lot of pressure but I guess what I'm
saying is just hang in there and keep dancing so good
because you totally saved us on this tour and this is
such a great opportunity for you and no matter what
I'm definitely going to get you another meeting with
don dezer after the tour is over but in the meantime it's
really important that you and darcy get along she really

talks about you all the time and considers you one of her closest friends, isn't that awesome to be best friends with a superstar, so anyway how are you? and besides if you get yourself fired I'll probably get fired too. is rashid still there I need to talk to him again."

I didn't even get in a single word, I just handed the phone back to rashid, who winked at me and said to eileen "let me call you back e.w." and hung up. he asked if I was gonna be cool and I said yeah then he gave me a huge hug, then he left. I locked the door behind him.

was that eileen's lame attempt at a peptalk? or was that some kind of apology? or was it a roundabout threat from darla, sent through eileen? or was it just eileen bugging out? I don't know. it's so hard to figure out what everything means around here.

evan just signed on. I don't have the energy to chat. i just really need to be alone right now.

SlipKnotRules933111: Kel?
KellyKelSoCal321 has signed off.

5onder

D-ZONE, 11:30 PM

Outfit: pjs and a wifebeater.
Mood: sleepy. hardly slept all night. went to the kitchen around 4 AM for a diet coke. Walter was there too. we waved at each other but didn't speak.

To: KellyKelSoCal321
From: SlipKnotRules933111
Date: Friday June 14
Time: 11:45 PM
Subject: whatsup
how come you just signed off on me?

I felt so bad when I read that. And now I have to tell him he can't come up this weekend. I can't deal with disappointing people, least of all him. that reminds me I need to set up an account to save money for his tuition at the martino school.

aaaaagh I am so stressing out right now. my brother hates me and I leave for my very first major world tour on Monday and darla barnes hates me and my mother's probably getting another divorce and my hair is getting more orange by the second (hello Shaundree) and my family is going to be broke if mom gets divorced. and not only that I have to dance my first major show ever in less than a week in front of 18,000 people. I mean if one dancer makes a mistake, it can throw everyone else off and if jesus and armand and the rest of them have been chilly to me up till now, I can only imagine the ice storm that would await a screwup like that.

on that encouraging note, I'll go see what's for breakfast and prepare to dance my ass off.

PLANE TO ST. LOUIS, 2:54 PM

Outfit: It's Darcy!! official tour jacket. just like all the other dancers on the plane. yep, we all have the same jacket on. nice huh. very broadway wannabe.
Hair: darcy offered to let me have shaundree fix it when we get to St. Louis. yes, we're really going. it's happening.
Mood: more dazed than confused, I think.
Fortune: Aim high.

---

leave it to me to puke on takeoff. I can't believe it. I am so bad on planes. it's embarrassing. there's something about the smell of puke, too, that never seems to go away. everyone on the plane hates you when you puke. like I'm SORRY but believe me I didn't WANT to puke! it's not like I planned to puke and ruin everyone's morning. god I wanted a parachute.

I was sitting by Darce but after I hurled she moved to another seat. some best friend, huh. ha ha.

I swear it was the takeoff. I did NOT puke due to nerves.

Oh did I mention the news? everyone's been squawking about how the "Cherry Red Lips?" video went to #1 on TRL this weekend. Pashmina's "My Needs Come First" was #2. Walter even made a special Hawaiian pineapple cake last night to celebrate. I'm going to miss Walter.

GRAND HOTEL, ROOM 813

ST. LOUIS, 11:45 PM

Outfit: same tour jacket as above.
Hair: I can't keep track anymore it changes so much.

I got my first taste of how weird this is really going to be when we were met at the airport today by like 5,000 screaming fans and at least fourteen TV cameras. there were like *thousands* of people there. ok maybe not but *hundreds* for sure. it was absolute MAYHEM.

Fans were *jammed* into the baggage area screaming "DARCY!! DARCY!!" and holding up signs like "Darcy Rules" and "Teamsters for Darcy" and "Thank U Darcy from St. Louis Virgin Alliance" and "Darcy I'm a Gigolo but I'll Do You for Free!" and stuff.

(what's a teamster, anyway?)

then there were these other signs at the back of the crowd: "Pashmina Is the Queen of St. Louis!" and "Just Say No to Lollipops!" and "Darcy Can't Sing" and stuff. (i could tell that the singing one got to her. she hates when people compare her voice to Pashmina's. let's face it, Pashmina is a much better singer. but Darcy's still a bigger star. guess singing doesn't really matter all that much, does it?)

we walked fast, all of us in sunglasses, surrounded by a team of men and women in black. Darcy and darla were arm in arm, gazing downward. I was way back with the other dancers, bringing up the rear, trying to coast under the radar and soak it all in, and these random faces would pop out from the crowd and scream "DARCY!!" right in front of us. it was such a trip. people were FREAKING and SCREAMING in our faces. not to be gross, but Darcy Barnes fans seem to generate a lot of saliva. I guess that's what antibacterial wipes are for.

and then there were all these really weird, really strange, totally silent fans who just stood there in our path staring at darcy with their mouths open and their eyes really wide. it was like they were paralyzed. they looked like what I imagine a stalker looks like, and they scared the hell out of me.

Of course, I was freaking out. my inner voice was squealing oh my god finally. just when I thought this whole experience was going to be a big bore, we're hit with a wall of paparazzi and crazy psyched-up fans. this is just like I pictured it. this is sooo celebrities uncensored. this is So E! True Hollywood story! I am fabulous!

but there was this other voice in me saying ok, here I am on TV for the first time and I'm wearing the same outfit as everyone else. we look like cheerleaders. wait, we basically are cheerleaders. we look like a bunch of dorks! the tinas were really into it, and d-run was eating it up, but I could tell angelina and I felt the same way. she and I bowed our heads and covered our eyes for a moment, but through my fingers I could see darla looking at me. she must love watching us squirm.

and there was this other voice in me saying, good thing no one's commented on my "fitness level" in a while or this could be a serious fat moment.

and another one saying, don't look at me! freakin' paparazzi leave me alone!! nobody look at me!

and a last one saying, look at me. look at me! this was the loudest one, so I started smiling.

through my teeth I realized I was still nauseous. maybe it was all the flashbulbs going off in our faces. I realized darcy was right in front of me. she turned to me, teeth gritted and big, and goes, "move. now." she grabbed my arm and we started power walking straight for the wall of flashbulbs. "we have to break through."

another side of darcy: the charlie's angel.

anyway so as we were racing through the airport these reporters kept screaming questions like, "So what do you have to say about the controversy?" and "How do you justify your decision?" and "have you responded to the offer for your virginity?" and stuff like that. Darcy and Darla and everyone just kept looking at each other like, controversy? What controversy?

the reporters kept on, kind of like chasing us through the airport. "What prompted you to make the decision to start your world tour in Pashmina's hometown?" and "Pashmina says she's shocked that It's Darcy!! is kicking off in St. Louis. but she calls it typical and she welcomes you to her hometown nonetheless. What's your response?" "Where's Jesse Nixon?" "Has your virginity status changed yet?" "Who are you wearing?"

So I guess Pashmina is from here. I wonder if Darcy even knows that. But then out of nowhere Eileen popped up and whispered something in Darcy's ear. She was obviously trying to do some damage control. Then Darcy stopped cold, and all of a sudden the entire room stumbles over itself, rights itself, and goes silent. she looks straight into the closest tv camera. all these random mikes appeared out of thin air, jammed in her face all at once like flies on a jar of honey.

she inhales, focuses, smiles big, and in a really loud, really clear voice with more twang in it than I'd heard before, goes, "Thank y'all so much for coming. Lordy what a great welcome! Thank you! We're looking forward to playing a sold-out concert for 18,000 of our fabulous St. Louis fans Friday night. We wish you could all be there, but the show just sold out so quick. I'm so sorry if you don't have tickets! Hopefully you'll learn to order early next time! Thank you again! My fans are just the greatest fans in the whole wide world! See you all Friday night!"

and then we left.

no one followed us after she finished speaking.

I was like wow, what a pro. she really knows what she's doing here.

KellyKelSoCal321: DUDE!

SlipKnotRules933111: what's going on I'm watching Cops this drunk guy is flipping off the camera.

KellyKelSoCal321: I'm in St. Louis. my first show's on friday.

SlipKnotRules933111: oh yeah. oh my god he just took a swing at the camera and his wife put her cigarette out on his car!

KellyKelSoCal321: I'm nervous.

SlipKnotRules933111: now their dogs are coming out of the trailer holy shit

KellyKelSoCal321: you know what evan. I love you. but you can be a jerk sometimes. will you at least say good luck.

SlipKnotRules933111: good luck.

KellyKelSoCal321: thanks.

SlipKnotRules933111: you don't need luck kel. you won't mess up. you're too good. hey did you puke on the plane?

he really knows how to melt me. I love that kid.

To: kaykay4real
From: Tito_T
Date: Monday June 17
Time: 11:45 PM
Subject: Reality check
Just a quick note because I have to get back to Sally Jessy. It's transvestite makeovers. But they just showed Darcy Barnes's "Aloha Thanksgiving" special

from last year on USA. That one where
she parasails in that pilgrim hat and
black-and-white tankini? Yes, they were
showing a Thanksgiving special in June.
Whatever, I totally watched and pictured
you in the next one. You're keeping some
pretty stylish company there, Kel!
I love you,
Teeto

I love you too, Tito.

we'll be practicing all week. we kind of took over the
whole concert arena for the next few days, using it to
work out the last little kinks in the show before we go
live on friday.

that's just 4 days away.

I wonder if Pashmina will be at the show. After all, it is
her hometown . . .

GRAND HOTEL

ST. LOUIS, 11:30 PM

Outfit: still wearing my encore costume (dress rehearsal today . . .): black sports bra and black square-cut boys' bathing suit.
Hair: someone get me some frizz ease, quick
Fortune: One slow, steady step at a time.

---

ok tomorrow's the show. I can't believe it. I'm freaking. I don't think I can do it. i'm going to blow it.

i can't believe they haven't fired me yet. especially after today. I practically ruined the whole show. ok let me explain.

we had a dress rehearsal today, which means we had to wear all six of our stage costumes, doing the changes and everything, and can I just say that I don't like any of the outfits except for the bolero jacket I wear for "Carpe Diem (Seize Me)" but anyway . . . we do it onstage, with all the correct lights, sound equipment, everything. basically it's a full-on live show without the audience. we were ONSTAGE at the arena, which is HUGE!

I mean, the biggest stage I ever shook it on was at last year's regional recital in front of like 200 people. so I've never danced with that many lights pointing directly into my face or in a place with that kind of sound system. it was almost like there was something wrong with it . . . there was tons of feedback and everything and I could see Jesse Nixon was sitting there just offstage watching us. I now officially think he's gross. I keep thinking about the way he was leching all over me on the couch in the pit.

Anyway, as much as I tried to stay loose and relaxed, my feet were starting to feel like they were made out of concrete or something and instead of dive rolling through Li'l D and armand's legs like I was supposed to, I dive rolled directly into their knees, causing a total domino effect and taking out all three dancers. legs and arms were everywhere. I landed directly on my face and I'm not just saying that. I seriously landed right on my face like, directly. and not only that, Li'l D then landed directly on my head. I don't want to overshare here but let's just say I got a superduper closeup of what tina's been dealing with over the last few weeks and, well, she must be some kind of circus freak. but anyway.

so the music just kept on going. "Whenever I fall / Whenever I call / Whenever I want you baby / You're there on your knees . . ." and we're all lying there in a heap in the middle of the stage. everyone else got up and stepped way back from me, like I had the plague. armand was actually *pointing* at me. I didn't even bother hoping that darla wasn't watching. I just *knew* that Darla was watching from somewhere, giving me the LOOK.

I closed my eyes and tried to disappear into the stage. then I felt rashid's hand on my shoulder. he helped me up and walked me aside, offstage, down into the front row. I was gasping for air and fighting back tears. humiliated didn't even begin to describe how I felt.

rashid looked me in the eye, holding my chin. "it's ok, girl. you just need to RE-LAX." I pulled my head back and go, RE-LAX?? are you KIDDING? hello I'm on the biggest stage in the universe and I can't see ANYTHING with these lights and I suck and this outfit is so not me and I feel like everyone's mad at me and now I'm totally scared to really dance, totally afraid to let myself go THERE. and did I mention I suck?

I really struggled hard not to cry. I just didn't want to be a crybaby right then. but I couldn't help it, my eyes started to water and I started to sob. I kept thinking god I hope everyone's not watching but I knew they were.

rashid just hugged me for a minute, told me it was all gonna be cool. and there was something about the feel of his arms that reminded me of dad and I just let it go. I didn't wail out or sob loud enough to entertain the entire arena. I kept it local. but I released a lot of tears into his arms. And rashid held me, tight, the whole time.

after a couple of minutes I suppose, or maybe ten, rashid lifted me up. he handed me a bandanna to wipe off my face and he asked how I'm doing. I said fine.

he said good because we have to get back up on that stage right quick before we get in any more trouble. and we both laughed. as we were walking back up he kept his arm around me, peptalking me the whole way.

he told me to not be afraid of being THERE, but to be careful with it . . . he told me how the hardest but most important thing to learn when you're a dancer isn't how to get THERE (although every dancer calls it something different), it's how to get THERE and *stay* THERE, to float, without losing any concentration or control. it's a conscious THERE, not a blind THERE if that makes any sense.

and, he added, Without injuring your fellow dancers.

that made me laugh.

I was like, everyone just watched me have a total nervous breakdown. rashid just kept saying "forget them. forget them. you're here to dance. just dance, k.k. forget the rest of it."

as I got to the stage darcy came over, looked me in the eye, and goes, "u ok?" and I was like yeah and she goes good. no extra-special hand squeeze or anything like that. just "good" and then she stood up and faced the company. "ok everyone let's take that one from the top. we gotta pull this show together. now."

we started from the top, had a clean run-through and a flawless sound check. thank god.

I was like ok, I can do this.

what a day. my head is throbbing. my stomach is out of control. I hope I can do this.

someone's at the door.

GRAND HOTEL

ST. LOUIS, 11:55 PM

Outfit: evan's Insane Clown Posse t-shirt again. I'm gonna sleep in it.

Hair: clean. they told me to wash it tonight, not tomorrow.

Mood: trying to just stay focused on tomorrow night. I CANNOT FUCK UP LIKE I DID TODAY.

---

that was darcy at the door. she said she's freaking out about tomorrow. she said she never gets used to doing shows, she's always convinced she's gonna screw things up, she hates the bolero jackets in carpe diem, her hair gets stuck in her mlke, what if those asymmetrical skintight white 80s jeans in the third section split up the back just like Jessica Simpson's did that one time in New York and that other time in Albany and everyone sees my ass, what if everyone's right and i really CAN'T sing, etc. etc.

she went on for like 30 minutes.

I was like damn! she gets stage fright! and I realized that whatever pressure I'm feeling, she probably feels even more. I felt for her. if I were her I would have needed a best friend right about then. so I went into best-friend mode. actually I went into coach mode. I was like girl you can *DO* this. you've been working so hard. dude you know this stuff! and not only that you told me yourself that once you get onstage in front of an audience you turn it up ten times higher and you always surprise yourself. you are gonna kill it tomorrow night!

thanks, she said. But you don't know what it's really like.

I go maybe I don't know what it's like to be the star, but this is my first big show ever, and I happen to be TERRIFIED. so I kinda DO know what it's like.

she goes "you? why would you be scared? you have it easy! you know what you're doing! you're way more talented than I am! you're a total natural! trust me, don't worry about it being your first show ever. you are the least likely of anyone to fuck it up, believe me! I'm not kidding. I know things like this. besides no one's coming to see you anyway. no one really cares about you. they're coming to see me. paying to see me. it's a lot of pressure."

I heard myself saying "you won't fuck up" but I was really thinking, um, was that supposed to be a compliment? and why are we talking about you again? but I just kept breathing and smiling at her.

then she goes "oh I almost forgot do you want anything on the rider contract?" I was like what's the rider contract. and she goes it spells out what we get backstage, like food and stuff. Then she handed me this paper. here's some of it. I had to read it over like two or three times before I really started to understand how ill it really is. check it out.

It's Darcy!!

The Darcy Barnes World Tour 2003

Technical Rider Contract

Item 7

Furniture and Settings for Darcy Hangout Room (not to be confused with Darcy Dressing Room) (1–2 people)

Three six-foot couches, two easy chairs, odor-free carpeted floor, large coffee table, two floor lamps, six folding chairs, cushioned. Please dress room up to make it feel like "home." (We encourage you to refer to Darcy's 2002 Christmas special, "Down the Chimney with Darcy," filmed at her childhood home in East Texas. Available on VHS from the Darcy Live! website.) Large TV with digital television service including all premium channels. Playstation 2 with several late-release games (to be approved by Jesse Nixon). One UNLISTED outgoing telephone line. Any incoming calls will result in a $40,000 fine payable in cash by the promoter.

Item 8

Furniture and Settings for Darcy Dressing Room (3 people) (not to be confused with Darcy Hangout Room)

Eight 12-foot hanging racks for clothes. Eight ironing boards. Eight professional steamers. Four hair and makeup stations with full-spectrum vanity lighting. Six three-way mirror stations. Surround-sound stereo. Fully stocked makeup and hair product cupboards (refer to item 26 for specific products and

133

please feel free to increase, or even double, recommended counts of lipgloss, mascara, and body glitter).

Item 9

Furniture for Band and Dancers Dressing/Hangout Room (16 people)

One six-foot couch, one coffee table, one buffet table, four folding chairs, cushioned or uncushioned. (Note: it doesn't really matter.)

Item 10

Furniture for Darla Room (1 person)

Queen-size bed. Bidet. Two eight-foot couches. Amber- or red-toned lighting. Body-lengthening mirrors (to be approved by Eileen Wang).

Item 11

Catering for Darcy Hangout Room (1–2 people)

24 one-liter bottles fresh spring water (NO bubbles)

1 quart-size Nantucket Nectars cranraspberry

1 case cans Coke.

4 bottles POWERade NOT grape

12 cans Red Bull

hot/cold water tank

3 tins General Foods International Coffees, Suisse mocha

4 boxes Xtra antioxidant green tea

fresh fruit platter

fresh veggie platter

cold bucket of KFC extra crispy. No potato salad or biscuits.

homemade banana bread from promoter. (Darcy's doing a search for the bestest in the country.)

two boxes Honey Nut Cheerios

large box of Jolly Ranchers, watermelon

1 extra-large bottle of Tums, assorted

appropriate napkins, glasses, utensils, etc.

Item 12

Catering for Band and Dancers Room (16 people)

1 small fruit tray, canned fruits

6 small bottles of spring water

6 small juices

4 cans soda (assorted)

1 small bag of corn chips

instant coffee

I was like wait, darla gets her own room, with a bed? but all sixteen dancers and band members share one couch and one small bag of corn chips?

what's a body-lengthening mirror and why does Eileen have to approve it?

but I didn't say anything like that.

she goes, "omigod don't think you're going to have to be in the dancers and band room. it sucks in there! no way, you're totally hanging with me in the Darcy hang-out room. I need my best friend there for all the press walk-throughs. it'll be fun we'll totally play video games! so anyway do you want me to add anything to this list? like do you have a kind of instant coffee you really like? and can I borrow that Insane Clown Posse t-shirt you're wearing?

and all I could think was

1. Great, it's not like the dancers don't hate me enough as it is. now I have to hang out with darcy instead of them.

2. Damn, now I'm never going to get a second to myself to try and relax before the show.

3. Oh God does this mean Darla's going to be on my case even harder?

4. Am I insane? Darcy Barnes wants me to share her hangout room! Like I would ever say no?!

5. Yeah, I'd like to add a few things to that list. like a plane ticket home.

6. No, you can't borrow evan's ICP tee.

luckily she got a page and was like OOH gotta go! before I could cave in and say anything like "sure you can borrow my t-shirt anytime you want."

KellyKelSoCal321: hey dude I'm wearing your ICP t-shirt.

SlipKnotRules933111: you took that?

KellyKelSoCal321: yeah oops sorry but I really like it.

SlipKnotRules933111: good luck tomorrow night.

SlipKnotRules933111: hello?

KellyKelSoCal321: thanks for remembering evan. I love you.

now I know I'll be able to sleep all right. evan does that.

one more day till opening night. one more day . . .

FRIDAY JUNE 21

FIRST SHOW, DARCY HANGOUT ROOM BACKSTAGE
ST. LOUIS, 7:45 PM

Outfit: the first outfit for the opening song, "Love You Like a Lollipop." it's like a gas station attendant coverall, which unzips and pulls off. underneath, asymmetrical tech bodysuit with red white and blue sequins.
Hair: orange extensions. they glued them onto me.
Mood: psyched. anxious, terrified, pumped, etc. etc. etc. there's not really a word for it.
Fortune: In horse racing, the starting line and the finish line are the same line. (HUH?)

To: kaykay4real
From: Tito_T
Date: Friday June 20
Time: 3:14 PM
Subject: You ROCK
Good luck tonight babycakes. You are totally going to rock. Just let it rip, bring Kelly, and everyone will love you. I'll be watching MTV news later to see how it went.
Teets

I love tito. ok, ok, ok, ok. ok. ok. no problem. ok. um, one hour until the show.

OK!!

I'm totally freaking out. ok no problem.

everyone's yelling. ok. here's what's up.

darcy and i just went to a preshow meet 'n' greet with her fans. darcy made me go with her cause she said people like to see her with her dancers. it's a publicity thing, she explained, so that everyone thinks everyone on the tour is like best friends. then she goes, "but don't worry you and I really ARE best friends." how about that.

she had to sit behind a desk for 45 minutes shaking hands and signing autographs and smiling at everyone. it was jammed with fans aged 9–14, moms, random guys probably looking to score, disposable cameras. JAMMED with people. they were sort of forming a line around the edge of the room up to our little desk to meet darcy.

she made me sit next to her. the whole time.

which meant that everyone asked me for my autograph, too. I just figured they were all caught up in the moment or something and bugging OUT that they were meeting her because who the hell would want my autograph?

I signed it different each time, mostly because I've never really settled on a signature before. I never really had an "autograph" to give.

while she was signing some kid's cast, I asked darcy, "why do they want my autograph?" she goes, "dude, don't ask me. I guess they think you're famous now."

I was like wow. I'm like "Almost Famous."

the average age was like 10, 11 years old. most of them were with their moms. most of them had won some kind of contest at some local radio station. they had to call in 1,000 times or something to win "VIP" access to Darcy. half of these girls were crying hysterically. half of them were like lit up, like they'd eaten too many pop-tarts. it's so weird. was I ever like that?

I don't have much time to consider that because I don't have much time left to live. well ok that's a little dramatic but I'm seriously a half-hour from going onstage and I'm not sure I'm going to make it through.

I can do this. I can do this. darcy's in her dressing room and I'm alone in her hangout room, which is a huge change from five minutes ago when this place was CRAWLING with like even more contest winners and entertainment tonight cameras and everyone. oh and also this whole crew of Pashmina fans who snuck in all these "This Is Pashmina's Palace!" and "At Least Pashmina Can SING" signs and everything. but when they realized darcy wasn't in here they all bailed on this room. guess I'm not THAT famous yet ha ha.

cool with me. I'll take any second alone I can get.

everyone's screaming and running around like wild just outside the door, not in a bad way just in that way that I guess I always pictured from backstage with the back-street boys specials and stuff. everything seems so urgent and stuff. chaotic. but it's like here it is the big debut and I should be enjoying it but what if I totally mess up my dive roll or something again? I mean, it happened yesterday. why wouldn't it happen today?

ok. I'm going to be fine. darla gave us all a peptalk: "ok everyone here we go, let's all have a great show, everyone looked great out there at dress rehearsal . . ." then she stared directly at me and said, "but we'll need as much luck as we can get, no matter how smooth everything is going. so let's pray for that. remember, no room for screwups. ever."

then she made us pray. which is cool and all, I mean, I understand the whole praying thing. I just hate it when someone else makes me do it. but whatever.

thanks a lot darla. and by the way, fuck off!

ok, ok. ok, um, it's gonna be awesome. I'm gonna kill it out there. I've gotta kill it out there. I can step up. just like dad. Good in a crisis. Remember? ok. um, ok.

Nice 'n Easy just hit the stage. that means we have 20 minutes.

GRAND HOTEL

ST. LOUIS, 11:25 PM

What can I say? we KILLED IT.

first of all, I have never seen that many people all in the same place at the same time before. well maybe I have but it was really scary. our dressing room had a window out into the parking lot, and there was seriously a traffic jam as far as you could see, winding away from the stadium. the parking lot was filling up section by section and streams of people were forming these thick lines leading out from the stadium deep into the lot.

anyway, it was 10 minutes to eight before I knew it. I could hear what's-her-name from Nice 'n Easy going into her mike, "Thank you so much! Thank you! Remember girls, be Nice! Be Easy! Be Nice 'n Easy!" and the crowd kind of clapped and "woo-hoooed" a little bit.

fifteen minutes later, we all took our places offstage for the big open.

here's how it works. the stage is pretty much bare except for a set of stairs leading up to a platform. there's a curtain, like gauzy and white, covering the platform, which is dark. us girl backup dancers are offstage to one end, the guys are on the other end. darcy's behind the curtain in

142

the middle of the stage but no one can see her. this really deep voice like darth vader or whoever that guy is who goes "This is CNN" comes over the loudspeaker: "ladies and gentlemen, prepare yourself for a journey to a special place, to a world where a boy can be a boy and a girl can be a girl. a place where music is the true language of love. ladies and gentlemen . . ." how idiotic is THAT? ha I kinda love it. anyway as he's saying that, this light comes up behind darcy and projects her shadow against the curtain making her look like 40 feet tall. she's got this pimp fedora hat on and a suit with a really big lapel and huge shoulder pads. it's kinda like Michael Jackson meets Carmen Electra only it's a 40-foot-tall shadow. anyway right then the voice goes, "ladies and gentlemen . . ." again, and darcy leans into a standing mike that is also a 40-foot-tall shadow and whispers, "It's Darcy." and all of a sudden this mad crazy mix of "Love You Like a Lollipop" comes on and she tosses her hat off and her hair starts flying and the crowd starts screaming almost like they're in a panic and we all come rushing out and start serving it up down in front of the stairway. (I also have to say that little "It's Darcy" bit is one of the only things that actually comes out of her mouth for most of the show. ok that's an exaggeration but not much. but to be fair, she's copped to it already. she's said publicly she sings every note except on songs where she's dancing around. guess what, there's only like one song where she's not dancing around. but I'm getting off track.)

so for the next 78 minutes we hit it HARD pretty much nonstop, no intermission. from "Love You Like a Lollipop" straight through "Keep It Poppin'" and "Carpe Diem (Seize Me)" and on and on.

There are five costume changes.

1. "Japanese Schoolgirl on Ecstasy." Thigh-high tights, teeny minikilts in electric-pink-and-blue plaid, white panties with hello kitty faces, knit hoodie boleros in gold, pigtails, chunky sneakers.

2. "Motorcycle." jeans, leather chaps, faux tattoo sleeves that make your arms look all tattooed, wifebeaters, heavy boots, slicked-back hair.

3. "Good Girl Gone Bad." 50s knee-length pencil skirts, tight cardigans, bobbed wigs, stilettos. We tear off our sweaters and wigs midway through "Whenever"—you know, that part where the beat goes up. Then we're in our heels, skirts, and bras.

4. "Midnight at the Oasis." gauzy Arabian pants, sandals, jewels in our navels, hair flying, veils. we looked like belly dancers. this was my favorite look for sure. it covered my ass ha ha plus you don't have to smile all the time when you've got that veil on. what a relief.

5. "Really Real." matching-but-not hip-hop gear. baggy denims, baseball caps, team jerseys (we usually wear jerseys for whatever baseball or basketball team plays for the city we're in. never football. wonder why . . .).

We totally hit every routine perfectly, there were no screwups at ALL. the crowd was SO into it . . . they were

144

screaming so loud for so long that it was really hard to hear the music sometimes, even though I was wearing those little earphones that pop stars are always fiddling with (which basically just plays the same mix that's being piped through the stadium's sound system). I did the dive roll move in "Whenever" with no problems. I pulled off every single transition easily. the only hangup was when my bra strap on my third outfit (the one for "Plucky") totally shredded backstage but luckily shaundree lent me hers at the last second. no one noticed.

I'm not sure if I ever really got THERE during the show, but I'm definitely sure I got pretty close a couple of times. I guess there was just too much going on for me to really let myself go.

but the exhilaration I got from the crowd was out of control. even though I knew the applause wasn't for me, specifically, it thrilled me. I was walking on air from the first beat and didn't stop until we'd finished both of our encores.

I finally got the hi fives I'd been looking for for weeks, from the Tinas, D-Run, and everyone else. we pulled it off, and we all knew it. I almost felt like I belonged. almost.

I headed back to darcy's hangout room and collapsed on the couch (she told me to go back there and she'd meet me in a few). I was exhilarated.

I was there only like two seconds when up on the closed-circuit tv (which had a live stream from the main stage) I saw Darcy come back onstage.

"Hold up everyone! Lordy what a show!" she yelled into the mike. "Don't leave yet! We've got one more song to sing, if y'all don't mind! Whattya think?" of course the whole place was like WOOOOOOH! I was like omiGOD am I supposed to be down there? did I forget a whole number that we're supposed to do?

or was this a real, bona fide encore?

then darcy goes, "Mama?" and omigod, darla walks out from backstage, carrying a MICROPHONE! I sank back into the couch, riveted and in semi-shock. darcy goes, "this is my beautiful mama, and we've got a new song we'd like to share with y'all." darla and darcy sat down on stools, facing each other. then the guitarist (his name is rob but everyone calls him Throb) came out and sat on a stool behind them. and he started playing, acoustic, the sappiest, most R. Kelly–ish melody I've ever heard in my life.

Mama Knows Best
(© 2003 Darla Barnes, Darcy Barnes)

Darcy:

Mama don't you know
Doesn't matter how much I grow
Mama you always know best
Mama I may be
A woman now, just look at me
But Mama you still know best

Chorus

Mama knows best when I'm lonely
Mama knows best when I'm blue

146

Mama knows best cause I'm still her baby
Mama knows what's best for you
Mama knows best, oh yes, Mama knows best

Darla:

Baby, don't you know
No matter how far you go
Mama always knows best
There may come a day, someday
When you say Mama go away
But even then, Mama knows best

Chorus

Both:

Don't ever forget that I'm yo' mama
Nothing can tear us apart, no mama
Do everything your mama says
Forever, forever, for-EVVVVVVVVVVER, Mama!

Chorus

(improvise to fadeout)

I'm totally going to vom.

as soon as the song ended, the stadium erupted. I guess all the moms there (which made up a good 25% of the audience, I mean, I guess they figured they couldn't let their third graders attend alone ha ha) really liked it. no duh, right? I mean, it's all about ignoring your own mind and just doing what your mother says.

and those kids scream at anything darcy says.

I was grossed out but only momentarily. I had a lot to think about. I mean, hello, it was my first show! and I didn't screw up! I pretty much rule!

anyway darcy came crashing into her hangout room right after the show. I figured I'd start squealing, just like that night in front of The Wizard of Oz, so I did.

I jumped up yelling, "awesome awesome you were amazing! we did it!" I went over to give her a hug.

and she practically pushed me off her. all snappy, "dude we JUST started. don't you get it? we have 60 more of these shows to go. you seriously need to grow up. let's get back to the hotel. I gotta crash."

and I go, "well that last song was really beautiful" and she goes, "you think that was MY idea? no way. that song is going to kill this show. god, k.k. can't you shut up for one minute? fuck!"

so I did. I shut up. she was cussing. I knew something was wrong. Ugh Darcy Barnes sometimes you suck. I was just sitting there thinking man, can't I celebrate for like a minute? didn't I have a friend who looks just like you a few minutes ago? I just made it through my first stadium show ever and I didn't blow it. in fact I killed it! I even congratulated YOU. and *I'm* the one who needs to grow up?

I wish I'd had the guts to say it all out loud but we went all the way back to the hotel in silence. I realized I was starting to count on her to be my friend, whether our friendship was just a publicity stunt or not.

thank god for tito. at least HE had some love for me.

To: kaykay4real
From: Tito_T
Date: Friday June 20
Time: 10:14 PM
Subject: Killer
Who killed it? You killed it!
Tee toe
PS—Are you at all responsible for this
"Mama Knows Best" fiasco?

I guess he'd heard about it on MTV news—they were there covering the show. Apparently they referred to it as the low point. anyway he also paged me like fourteen times:

> *U ROK! WORSHIP U! >3>3 >3*

and

> *KELS DA MAN!!!*

and

> *MISS U DIVA*

and

> *T-To LUVS U*

etc. etc. etc.

he rules.

GRANDE ALL-SUITES HOTEL

KANSAS CITY, 11:36 PM

Outfit: terry robe.
Hair: sweaty and disgusting. I gotta take a bath.
Fortune: The road is shorter than you think.

---

tonight's show was even better than last night's but that is SO beside the point. The real news is that after the show, I was leaving the stadium with darcy and jesse and rashid. rashid was telling us this story about how darla fired latrell the makeup artist after the show tonight because she thought he had said something rude about her skin tone and now eileen was going to have to find someone by, like, tomorrow when the show was going to be in another city and what if they sucked and blah blah blah. anyway on our way out the back door to the car that was waiting to take us back to the hotel there was this one news guy with a camera pointed straight at us. and then this reporter pops out from behind him and sticks a mike into darcy's face and goes, "So, how long have you and Jesse Nixon been an item!"

we all stood there staring at this guy for a second and before I knew what was happening darcy just goes, "We are NOT an item! Lordy! We are just really great friends. I am so sure! right Jesse?" and he was like "yeah" then she grabs my shoulder and pushes me in front of her over next to jesse and goes, "Jesse is so not my boyfriend. He's dating my very

150

bestest ever friend K.K. here! Oh my Lordy! Aren't they just the cutest? Awww. Now can you leave us all alone?"

the reporter and camera dude kind of shrank back into the shadows.

Then she broke out her cell phone. "Hey, Eileen? How were the revenues tonight? What are our totals?"

I was like, wait, what? I'm dating *WHO??*

I looked over at Jesse, who just licked his lips and smiled at me. I realized that my fantasy was coming true: I was finally dating Jesse Nixon, just as I'd dreamed of a million times before and it was precisely NOT what I wanted. he took the opportunity to put his arm around my waist. ugh.

darcy made me ride on her bus last night all the way to Kansas City. she said she wanted to hang out with jesse and k.k., her two best friends, but it soon became pretty clear that I was her cover . . . she wanted to be with jesse, and I was just around to keep people from asking questions.

I got no sleep and I pretty much confirmed in every way but visually that jesse and darcy are way, WAY more than friends. her little cabin on the bus has a door, and it closes. she and jesse were behind it all night.

I'm no expert and I'm sure I could be wrong but, well, let's just say I heard things. if I didn't know better I'd say there's no way that anyone in that cabin was a virgin. But she says she's a virgin so that's pretty much that.

Oh man, I need tito. this is all way too ill for one person.

GRANDE ALL-SUITES HOTEL

KANSAS CITY, 11:55 PM

I'm nauseous. I was just watching jesse on a "total dedication show." he closed by saying he'd like to do his own dedication. and he introduced Darcy's new single by saying "this one's for you, K.K." here's the song.

View from the Top

(© 2003 Darcy Barnes Music)

Boy you know it's true
When I'm all over you
Ain't nothing you can do
Just keep on doin' what you do (Do it!)
Cause the view
From the top
Makes me pop
(Oooh yeah)
When I'm on top boy
You bring me so much joy
It makes me want to scream
Makes everything a dream
Cause the view
From the top
Makes me pop
(Oooh yeah)
[Bridge]

Don't try to hide
Just come inside
Baby you know you got it like that
Cause the view
From the top
Makes me pop
(Oooh yeah)
Cause the view
From the top
Makes me pop
(Oooh yeah)

(Repeat three times to fadeout)

I was like EW. I cannot believe he just dedicated that song to me in front of the whole planet.

GRANDE ALL-SUITES HOTEL

KANSAS CITY, 2:01 PM

Fortune: Who do you think you are?

To: kaykay4real
From: Tito_T
Date: Sunday June 23
Time: 1:11 AM
Subject: You're (in)famous
What's THIS about?? I found it online.

BAD NEWS AGAIN, GIRLS

Seems Darcy "Plucky" Barnes and Jesse "VJ du Jour" Nixon are off again for the moment, but the reason is rather shocking. Seems Jesse's been swapping spit with one of Darcy's backup dancers, one K.K. Kimball, a newish dancer straight outta San Diego. (Which is about all we know about her.) But wait, there's more. Sources say Darcy's the one who introduced the new duo, and she's even been quoted as saying she thinks they look "adorable" together. Yep, a local news reporter from St. Louis WWQW-TV caught Darcy on camera gushing over the couple, saying, "Aren't they just the cutest?" So what gives? We're wondering if the Darce-meister is clearing the way for a new romance. Or maybe Jesse's been pressing her to reconsider her virgin

status? You know we'll keep you posted ... After all,
Jesse Nixon's relationship status is do-or-die news
for us, too!

oh god, this isn't happening. this can't be happening.
oh god. I wrote back:

To: Tito_T
From: kaykay4real
Date: Sunday June 23
Time: 8:54 am
Subject: over my head!
Tito that's not even half of it.

KellyKelSoCal321: dude did you hear anything about me online or anything?

SlipKnotRules933111: ???

KellyKelSoCal321: I heard there were some
rumors online but they aren't true

SlipKnotRules933111: ok. I have no clue
what you're talking about but whatever.

KellyKelSoCal321: I'm freaking out.

SlipKnotRules933111: whatever. look I'm freaking too. carl told mom that he's been seeing
that other woman. the twins have met her and
everything. but he said he wants to stay to
work it out or whatever.

KellyKelSoCal321: how do you know

SlipKnotRules933111: they fought about it
in the yard last night right outside my
window

KellyKelSoCal321: oh man, what did she say

155

SlipKnotRules933111: nothing she just went to bed

KellyKelSoCal321: is she losing it?

SlipKnotRules933111: I don't know I haven't seen her.

KellyKelSoCal321: where's carl now?

SlipKnotRules933111: I don't know he's not here though.

KellyKelSoCal321: are the girls there?

SlipKnotRules933111: I don't think so.

KellyKelSoCal321: you don't think it's just another one of their spats or whatever

SlipKnotRules933111: I don't think so. hey did you watch When Good Cops Go Bad last night?

DARCY'S BUS

ON THE WAY TO DES MOINES, 9:18 PM

Outfit: It's Darcy!! tour jacket, track pants, slip-on sneakers.
Mood: incredulous. (I looked it up.)

I can't sleep, so I'm writing. I'm trying to stay as cool as I can, but I'm definitely freaked out about everything. I mean can you blame me? the sucky part is I don't feel like there's anyone here I can really talk to about everything. I mean I can talk to rashid about some stuff and darcy about some stuff and even like eileen about some stuff but there's no one I can put it all together with. I miss tito.

after managing to keep my head down all day, darcy finally cornered me, dragging me onto her bus for the overnight haul to Des Moines. We were sitting in front of the flat screen eating contraband chocolate when darcy hit the mute button.

How do you like my new bangs? she asked, flipping her freshly cut bangs.

I was like, huh? um, they're great! I tried to muster a squeal, no luck.

"look," she goes. "I know you're bugging about this whole thing with you and jesse and the press and everything, but don't worry. believe me I know it'll all blow

157

over and in a few weeks pretty much no one will remember you. I promise. they'll be like 'Kelly who?' Oh, uh, um, well that didn't sound right but you know what I'm trying to say."

I was like I guess so. I mean she's been through this kinda stuff a lot, right? so she would know. right? she goes, "it's like that time when I was banned in Singapore or wherever it was because they said I was a bad influence. you just gotta let people talk about you for a while and ignore it. it's the only way." I was like, well, not really, but ok.

I was also like well yeah this "whole jesse thing" is bugging me out, but there's a lot more that's bugging me out, too. but you wouldn't know. It's stuff you wouldn't understand. and I don't really want to talk about it, so I won't.

she goes, like what?

and I go, nothing. seriously.

and she goes, you mean you're bugging about me and jesse and what our deal is?

and I go, no, not really.

so darcy pulls this picture out of her bra and hands it to me. it's her and jesse, arm in arm. "ok first of all I have a little eensy secret. remember how I was saying that I had a boyfriend that one night? well, um, it's Jesse Nixon. we've been going out for a while."

my first thought was, no kidding. I'm surprised you can

walk after last night's bus ride! but I didn't say it out loud. I forced myself to giggle. she goes, "What?" and I was like, "nothing." and she goes, "what, did you guess?"

and I was like, "believe it or not, I wasn't sure." I was kind of lying but something told me it was ok in this case. "I mean I heard it but I didn't buy it. but I think it's totally cool. it's true you guys really *are* perfect together. perfect. just look at you." I pointed to the picture. I didn't really believe they were perfect together now that I'd actually been introduced to Jesse Nixon, but I knew she'd want to hear it.

and she goes, "yeah we are, aren't we? he is sooo cute! we are the cutest! but it totally sucks because it's really important for our careers that we both stay single, you know. like how would all those screaming girls feel if he was off the market and I was the one who took him off it? they'd hate us both, especially me."

so instead they'll just hate ME, now that I'M supposedly the one who snagged him, I was thinking.

"so here's what I'm thinking. you can be his 'official' girlfriend, or someone he's dating or something, and that'll explain why he's around all the time. it'll totally make you famous and the press will ignore him and me. plus to make it even more clear, I'll just act like I'm totally head-over-heels-in-love crushing on Rashid, but he's just a little too old for me plus he's on the payroll. hello, I don't date dancers like that Pashmina does. no. anyway, jesse and I will get to stay together

159

and the best part is, my number-one crush/boyfriend-on-reserve stays off the market. ha ha. just in case I need a backup. don't you love it? isn't it like perfect?"

actually, I was thinking, not REALLY. It made me feel like her puppet or something. but what was I going to do? say no?

I think she could tell I was annoyed.

"what do you think?" she asked. "what's wrong?"

I go, "I don't know, Darcy. this is kind of a lot to think about. it kind of puts me in a weird position. I mean I don't know . . ."

she goes, I know. k.k., this is all crazy for me, too. I never know if I'm making the right decisions. ugh. I don't know. sometimes I think I'm just crazy. am I crazy?

she looked so young right then. no, I said. I don't. you're in a difficult situation. and now so am I. And then I groaned.

She grinned at me and I have to say it was kinda cute. it made me feel like protecting her.

ok, what if I also make you official lead dancer of the company? she said. You can be listed first on the programs and everything but you won't have to deal with any REAL responsibilities.

really? I didn't even know there was such a position. "no that's cool darcy, I don't want to take anyone's position away" and she goes, "no, I just made the position

160

up! I can do that! I'll make eileen announce it to the press this week. what do you say?"

what could I say? I couldn't just say no. tito would kill me if I did that. so I just gave a little squeal. she goes "cool! then it's settled! hey want to watch The Little Mermaid? I have the DVD!"

then she goes, "and by the way, the part about me being a virgin? That part's totally true. jesse and I have never . . ."

CHICAGO, 10:05 PM

Outfit: army tee, pink hanes her way panties.
Mood: Feeling like I'm on TV all the time . . . everything seems so fake. Or maybe it's me?

Jesse showed up again tonight. it's so weird how he just pops up every now and then. it's like, don't you have a job?

the sucky part about it is whenever he shows up I have to be his girlfriend. remember? yeah, I'm his official girlfriend. that means darcy and I have to get a big suite with at least two bedrooms so he can sneak from my room to hers. funny how he always manages to flash me before he leaves "our" room. I've seen front and back at least three times by now. it's annoying. he's one horny dude. I wonder how darcy can keep up. anyway lately I've been locking him out after he leaves.

But the situation is totally worth it. I mean, hi, we always get the best room in the hotel. And there's really no lack of privacy for me. It's a pretty sweet deal. Also she pays for all the phone charges so I'm able to call tito and evan and everyone.

tonight darcy had to do a little "behind the scenes" interview for MTV Asia, so jesse came with me when I went back to the suite. after I let us in, I just pointed toward the door to darcy's bedroom and was like

162

"that's darcy's room. I'm raiding the minibar and crashing out. good night dude."

and he comes up to me, puts his arms around my waist, and goes, "hey is that any way to treat your official boyfriend?"

I just fake-laughed and squirmed out of his arms. he grabbed me again. "come on. you gotta feel the spark too, k.k. you're fine, I'm fine, we're fine. we should do what fine people do!"

he started slow dancing, singing "I wanna rock with you . . . all night" like Michael Jackson. I go, "dude, never, no way, you're darcy's boyfriend, and besides . . . here's a tip from the real world: that song will kill a girl's mood every time. you gotta get better material."

freak. It's amazing to me how someone I've obsessed about for so long, someone who occupied my daydreams for so long, could be so totally unattractive as he is right now. It's like he's got this thing where he thinks everyone wants him   like all he has to do is wink at you and you'll melt.

I pushed his hands down and off me and went about my business. he just sat there all hurt. "come on baby, don't break my heart like that." I said, "give it a rest man. your girlfriend's on her way back here! and that puppy dog thing you guys do never, ever works on me."

he goes, "damn" and grabs the remote. He sat on the couch and proceeded to ignore me, which was fine.

there was nothing in the minibar so I just decided to get in bed. I shut the door to my room and grabbed my laptop.

CHICAGO, 11:03 PM

Mood: I feel like I did something dirty even though I didn't.
Hair: I just smelled it. I need to wash it.

---

ok ew I'm officially nauseous. I have made myself sick.

I fell asleep before I really got to writing before, but I got woken up when I heard darcy come back to the suite. I could smell pot, I guess it had come in under the door.

right away jesse was like, "where the hell have you been? I've been waiting for like two hours" and darcy was like, "what are you talking about? I just did my interview and came straight here! and it looks like you're having an OK time without me, stoner!"

and he was like, "damn I can't believe you made me wait so long!"

neither of them said anything for a few minutes, then I could make out muffled voices.

I heard them go into darcy's bedroom and close the door. I heard the lock go, too.

then I got really dawson's creek about the whole thing. I actually put my ear up against the wall and listened. her bed was pushed right up against the wall, I guess, cause I could hear a lot. now I don't want to make this an x-rated diary or anything but let's just say I heard jesse nixon and darcy barnes make out, get stoned, and engage in, what do they call it in junior high?

oh yeah, *heavy petting*.

I didn't pull my ear away until I heard jesse say, "are you done baby? hold on. lemme go get a towel."

I'm going to need lifelong therapy.

INDIANAPOLIS (I think), 3:05 PM

Outfit: I tried to board the bus in just my tank top but Darla glared at me so I put on my tour jacket. I was sweating all day.
Hair: Never better. Shaundree touched up my roots.

Sorry I haven't written in so long. I guess you could say I've been having the time of my life. Six shows a week, but lots of time to just hang out too. Mostly with darcy, but also rashid, who's gone from my crush to my friend and poker pal. He calls me the shark. I can thank my dad for that one—he taught me all I know about five-card stud.

I swear every town we get to has more screaming fans than the last one. and what's really tragic is the deeper we get into summer, the hotter it gets, the less people in the audience are wearing. and here's a rule that everyone should have to learn: just because your pop idol looks cute in a sports bra and track pants doesn't mean that you do. and all those ill signs: "Lipstick Me" "Virgin and Proud" and "Darcy It's My Birthday!" and the scariest: "Moms United for Darla and Darcy." today someone even came up to darcy and goes "I named my baby after you will you bless her?" and darcy goes "I don't think I'm allowed to do that."

ooh evan just signed on.

KellyKelSoCal321: do you get any summer vacation at all?

SlipKnotRules933111: yeah next week mom's making me go to palm desert to visit Aunt Linda.

KellyKelSoCal321: oh god no.

SlipKnotRules933111: yes. I really don't want to go to the desert. I really wish she'd just let me stay here

KellyKelSoCal321: no way then you'd be in twin hell

SlipKnotRules933111: I could hide

KellyKelSoCal321: what if I asked her to let you come to Orlando? we're going there tomorrow to do two shows there then we're shooting a new video for "Wax On, Wax Off" then we get two days off so we'll be there for like two weeks . . . you could come for practically the whole time.

SlipKnotRules933111: what would I do there

KellyKelSoCal321: I don't know just hang out. ask mom if you can come here instead. I'll buy your ticket

I know I'm supposed to be saving money or whatever but I can get him a plane ticket. maybe I can even use one of the vouchers continental airlines gave us all. they're helping sponsor the tour or whatever. besides, I'm having a blast. he'd have a blast. he and darcy love each other. he should come up.

DARCY'S HOUSE

ORLANDO, 9:30 AM

Outfit: darcy's t-shirt, darcy's track pants, darcy's scrunchie.
all my stuff's in the laundry or something.
Fortune: Follow the signs.

Darcy woke me up this morning by jumping on my bed.
well, not really my bed. I've been sleeping in darcy's hot
older brother's bed. don't worry he's out of town.

yeah, she has a house down here. you pretty much can't be
a teen pop star without a spread within range of disney
world, know what I mean? a couple of the guys from the
Backstreet Boys or one of those old boy bands live down
the block—a couple of the guys, not a "couple couple," er,
whatever. I'm sure the Lacheys have a spread nearby. maybe
Aaron Carter, too. oh and darla has her own place. it was
her way of giving darcy and her brother some "space" or
her way of giving herself some space. or something.

so we're down here for a couple of weeks or so to take
a break before heading up to New York, where darcy's
agreed to do a pay-per-view show. (of course, that
includes yours truly . . .) it'll definitely be the biggest
show of this tour, and everyone is starting to get pretty
revved up about it. I'd rather chill out though, ya know?
this is our big chance to relax . . .

Anyway so yeah darcy started jumping on my bed

before I even knew what was up. I go, "What the fuck is going on?" (I can be like that in the morning some-times . . . cranky as hell. I think I get it from my mother.) and she goes, "relax! jeez, so cranky! we have to watch the today show! jesse is going to be on!"

and she cranks on the TV. it's Pashmina singing "Working Girls" with Gwen Stefani, Beyonce, and Foxy Brown. darcy screamed out loud. EW! she covered her mouth with her hand and looked closer. under her breath I heard, "oh, my, god. look at how much makeup she has on!"

she was right. Pashmina looked like a clown. not like the cute kind, but like the scary kind that keep children up at night. and she was wearing panties that showed, well, pretty much everything. hello, camel toe!

CHANGE IT!! I screamed. she began pushing buttons frantically.

and there's katie couric staring out at us talking about west nile disease.

I go, Aren't you and your mom going to be on the today show one of these days?

she goes, No, that was the view, and it was last week. we flew up for a couple of hours when we were in D.C.

I go, Oh, I didn't know.

it sucked, she said. we had to sing mama knows best. she was silent for a minute.

i was about to say something lame like "that's cool"

when she started talking again. You know, it was our second time on the view this summer. I guess it's a record . . . The Star said it's the first time a mother-daughter team has performed the same song on the view twice.

I looked at her, wondering what to say. I had no idea if what she'd just told me was a good thing or not. I still hadn't figured out what to say during the LAST awkward silence and here I was faced with another one!

saved again! darcy blurted: "Hey! Why don't you and ME do a duet?"

I was like, um, ok, hell yeah! d.b. wants to do a duet, I'm down. like mama knows best? I said.

she goes NO way! You know I hate that song!

I was like PHEW! I HATE IT TOO! I laughed, and she laughed back.

This was one of those times when I actually liked her.

we'll make it about best friends. like you and moi! c'mon let's go down to my home recording studio!

I was like "home recording studio? what is this, MTV Cribs? ok. totally let's do it. hey you watch for jesse and I'll just take a quick shower ok??"

but she didn't hear me, I don't think. Katie Couric was talking about how this kid was rescued from a flood in Mississippi and darcy was totally crying. oh my lordy that is so sad! that little boy lost his puppy! oh I'm calling eileen to send him a new bloodhound. where's my cellie? Note: new addition to my list of her multiple personalities. Random Acts of Kindness Darcy.

I snuck down into her kitchen to see if there was any coffee brewing. rock and roll, there was.

I could hear her yelling upstairs: "K.K. you gotta see this! jesse looks sooo cute!"

I pretended not to hear. I focused on my coffee. It's not like we'll actually be writing a song together anyway. darla would never let that happen. there's no way darcy's serious about it.

O-TOWN, BABY, 12:15 PM

Outfit: I'm in the same thing I was in yesterday. everything darcy's. we haven't left the house and I haven't showered in over a day, and it feels great. :-)
Mood: After a rocky start, beginning to feel comfortable in this style to which I've become accustomed.

---

turns out darcy *was* serious about writing a song together.

see?

Be with Me (Reality)
(© 2003 Darcy Barnes and K.K. Kimball)

Don't be lame
Don't be stupid
Don't be boring
Don't be fake
Be real!
Don't be ill
Don't be crazy
Don't be shady
Don't be late
Be real!
You gotta be real
To be with me (reality)
You gotta know the deal
To be with me (reality)

Cause reality
Is the way to be
Be with me (reality)
Don't be a clone
Don't be trendy
Don't be just like
All the rest
Be real!

(Rap)

Reality reality is the only way that I can be
And all my girls around me say
Be real, be real, just keep it real, hey!
You gotta be real
To be with me (reality)
You gotta know the deal
To be with me (reality)
Cause reality
Is the way to be
Be with me (reality)

we finished it in like an hour and it was pretty cool. I went in just expecting to goof around and do silly stuff, but darcy went totally pro when we got into the studio. I was amazed at how well she worked that studio. it was pretty big . . . way bigger than Snoop's on Cribs. walls and walls of equipment and speakers and woofers and subwoofers and whatever else that stuff is. and like a soundproof booth with a big huge mike in it and a bunch of instruments leaning up against the wall.

darcy's a better musician than they give her credit for. that girl can play a tune on the keyboard by ear, no problem, even if when you hum it for her you're totally off-key. and she comes up with some really cute melodies. I found harmonies pretty easily for her melodies (thanks dad for that early childhood California Dreamin' training) and our voices didn't sound that bad together at all!

as far as lyrics, she said we should go for straight-out cheese because as far as she can tell, cheese is what sells. and she said she wanted me to make some money off of it. I was like, well, ok. why not. so cheese we produced.

she goes ha! I bet Pashmina can't write her own songs. and she didn't make the 50 most gorgeous list either did she? do you think my hair is better than hers?

luckily, my pager cut her off.

DUDE WHERE R U

DUDE WHERE R U

DUDE WHERE R U

etc. oh god not again. it's evan! it's 12:15, and he landed an hour ago. he's at the airport! luckily darcy keeps a navigator at this house, too. my brother needs a ride.

DARCY'S HOUSE

ORLANDO, 8:14 PM

Outfit: vintage OP long-sleeve tee, cargo shorts, flip-flops. I'm like the original surfer today.
Hair: shinier than ever. darcy and I soaked our hair in tea yesterday and lay out in the sun all afternoon. it really works! my calves got kinda sunburned though.
Mood: stoked to see evan. Note use of "stoked," a popular surfing expression. in fact, I'm in a good mood all around.

Evan was starving when we went to pick him up so we stopped off at hardee's drive thru, then dunkin' donuts. Then it was off to Disney World where we went through the VIP entrance for every ride.

we went on all the rides. it's amazing how, if you don't have to wait in line, you can really do all of them in a couple of hours.

evan and I got hardly three minutes alone the whole day to talk about mom. but he told me that she told him that she really wants to leave carl. that was right before she went to palm desert. I bet she's asking Aunt Linda for some money or if she and evan can stay there and if I know Aunt Linda she's saying no way you made this bed now you gotta sleep in it and then I can picture mom practically begging Aunt Linda and her still saying no.

and then I can picture mom totally bolting and giving up on the whole thing and crying in the car on the way home to san diego, alone.

damn I hate how money screws up everything. what am I going to do when this job is over?

RIHGA ROYAL HOTEL

NEW YORK CITY, 11:46 PM

Outfit: Shiny black halter and faded jeans. Black boots.
Hair: Just when I thought it couldn't get any better, Shaundree gave me this cocoa butter stuff that makes it so shiny. And it's back to light brown with blond streaks. she took a pic with her digital camera so I could email tito. he'll be so happy. but I digress.
Fortune: Do what needs doing. Don't do what doesn't.

---

oh, to be back in Orlando, back when Darcy wasn't so high maintenance.

ok here's my story. we are in new york for the biggest show on the tour, the one we're filming for a pay-per-view concert. everyone's sort of been talking about it since the beginning of the tour but I've been kind of not thinking about it. for me, every show is a big scary monster to face down . . . the new york pay-per-view show is just a little bigger and a little scarier . . . ok, it's a lot scarier. because I know tito will be watching. not to mention my mother. not to mention the entire rest of the world.

and tonight the record company rented out this bar called Jaguar or Leopard or something and threw her a huge party tonight for selling a trillion copies or what-ever. even though we knew we have a huge show com-ing up, *the* show, we partied pretty hard.

someone should tell darcy that she still can't legally drink. that would be fun. then again, she probably wouldn't pay much attention at the moment considering she's, well, *drunk* isn't really the word for it . . . Darcy barnes, the biggest star in the universe, the envy of teen girls everywhere and the x-rated daydream of teen boys everywhere is lying in the bathroom, wrapped around the toilet in a fetal position, refusing to stand up. or is it unable to stand up? . . . her head's wedged in kinda tight behind the plumbing back there. for all I know she could be immobilized. but maybe that's a good thing so she doesn't get in bed and puke *THERE* instead.

really attractive. very nice, for america's sweetheart.

it's amazing how, even in this position, she looks like she's posing. even in this position, her belly button is front and center. the girl can't even puke without her belly showing. did she PLAN that? hair crusted with vomit notwithstanding, she's camera ready.

Yup, crusted vomit. well, I guess that's what she gets for slamming down 4 slippery nipples in a half-hour at Deep, THE club this week in nyc. (yes, if you're a celeb, you *can* get a drink before age 21. in fact, if you even know a celeb, you can get a drink. how do you think I got my own slippery nipple? notice I said one. which I didn't even finish. not four.)

anyway, so yeah, darcy downed four slippery nipples before they even served the cake. yeah, *that* cake. it was a "photo-frosted" cake that was iced to supposedly look like her face in the "Love You Like a Lollipop" video but instead it looked like courtney love meets marilyn manson.

anyway, there she was, drunk in a coochie-slit skirt and a deep-neck crop jacket (no shirt), bending over to blow out candles that weren't even there. she thought it was her birthday, I guess. either that or she'd WANTED to give the front of the room a boob show and the back of the room a butt show.

talk about your slippery nipples! and hello, I see London and France. Hell, from this angle I can see Lake Titicaca.

out of the corner of my eye I also caught jesus and armand engaged in a full-on tongue kiss.

luckily (I guess) no one really captured the critical moment for major worldwide circulation. at least, not that I saw. I mean, I guess seeing paris hilton's was enough for one summer and the paparazzi decided it was no longer a scoop. or maybe the paparazzi were too busy drooling to get their cameras focused in time. sickos. the girl is barely legal.

She's moaning in there. she just goes, "jesse, jesse." Yeah I WISH jesse was in town right now. Then I wouldn't have to deal with this. you would have passed out on his watch, not mine. The thing is you never really know when he's going to be around and when he isn't. Guys.

Why isn't rashid here? He'd know what to do.

Should I go look and see how she's doing? Ugh. why

does this happen to me? ugh once again K.K. gets suckered into being darcy's best friend and watchdog. cause no one else will. (or no one else cares enough.)

especially not darla, who was busy the whole party, making out with some Man in Black in one of the back banquettes at the leopard or jaguar or whatever bar, and jesse had long since left with Outkast and Tara Reid, and rashid wasn't even there, so the only person there to rescue darcy from herself was you guessed it, moi. I had to get her out of there. I mean it's not like darcy can be seen staggering drunk from her big fancy industry party all alone, looking around for her car or something. I sucked it up and we ducked out, me smiling and darcy drooling. I tried my best to hold her up. she tripped on the curb, though, and at least one camera got her midfall. then she flipped off the assembled press from inside the car. I grabbed her hand to stop her.

It was a short ride back to the hotel, but she still managed to puke in the limo. make that on my boots. it was when this Pashmina song "Get Down on Me" came on the radio. I had to yell at the driver TURN THAT DOWN PLEASE but the damage had been done. she slurred Sssssshcrew Pashmina . . . ssshhhee can't sssssinnng . . . waitlllll my sssshow tomorrow night. you'lll seeeee. I'm going to ssssssing way better than pa-pa-Pashmina.

we finally made it back up to my room, Darcy draped across my shoulders, but not before she got all wack on me in the elevator and started talking about how much she loves me and admires me and how much I'm her best friend blah blah blah. I hate how she gets like that sometimes. (funny how it always happens after too many rounds of Peach Pussycats, Tequila Mockingbirds, or Cockblockers or something.)

anyway the poor li'l international superstar was halfway through her third "and I really want my hair just like yours. I mean, I don't CARE what it looks like!" when she sat down on the bathroom floor "just for a second." That's the last thing she said.

it's not pretty at the moment but whatever. the way I see it, we're in this together now, and she needs my help. besides I kinda owe her. she was so cool with my bro last week.

should I go in there? god this sucks.

SlipKnotRules933111: where are you

KellyKelSoCal321: new york

SlipKnotRules933111: carl and the twins are gone

KellyKelSoCal321: WHAT?

SlipKnotRules933111: left last night

KellyKelSoCal321: fuck. but do u and mom get to stay at the house?

SlipKnotRules933111: no he's coming back in four weeks and we have to be gone. we have until August 22

KellyKelSoCal321: where's mom

SlipKnotRules933111: she and that lawyer are talking downstairs.

KellyKelSoCal321: they spend a lot of time together

SlipKnotRules933111: tell me about it

KellyKelSoCal321: fuck, evan that sucks.

SlipKnotRules933111: that's ok I'm leaving tomorrow for a weeklong school trip to boot camp in utah.

KellyKelSoCal321: no WAY!

SlipKnotRules933111: yeah just like on Real Boot Camp Disasters!

KellyKelSoCal321: be careful dude ok

SlipKnotRules933111: you too

KellyKelSoCal321: what do you mean?

RIHGA ROYAL HOTEL

NEW YORK CITY, 6:50 AM

Mood: stressed out. they're coming at me from all sides. and tonight's the big pay-per-view show.

---

darla barnes pounded on my hotel suite door this morning at 6:30 AM and shoved a clipping from the New York Morning Star Herald-Tribune Post in my face. Doesn't she sleep?

Just asking . . .

Which overfeted multiplatinum-selling blond divette who's in town to shoot a much-hyped pay-per-view concert special and needs to be at the top of her game tonight toppled off her platform boots on her way out of last night's 18th birthday bash at a hip downtown nite spot? Seems the wasted warbler, in town to film a pay-per-view concert at the Garden, threw back an extra Slippery Nipple or two without considering the consequences (ah, the travails of youth) and after two bar-top dances and one involuntary flash had to be assisted (some say carried) from the venue by her bestest backup dancer, who lovingly deposited the soda-pop star back at their hotel before commencing yet another liaison with her paramour, himself a pop star of platinum status. Oh, and note to the porn star . . . we mean pop star . . . in question: you left your wrap at the coat check.

"HOW could you let this happen?" she screamed. "I trusted you with her last night. it was my understanding that you would not leave her side. you knew it was the night before the biggest show of the tour, the biggest show of darcy's life, yet you managed to get my daughter drunk in a bar? in front of industry people? what are you thinking?"

I thought about fighting back, defending myself. I thought about asking her what she was doing in that back banquette while her own daughter was abusing alcohol and inviting photographs of her panties, but I knew that would go nowhere. I just said, "I'm sorry."

she barked at me. "SORRY doesn't really cut it right now does it? Just be glad it was a blind item with no names. Oh, and I've granted an interview to the paper, in which I name you, k.k. kimball, as a bad influence on darcy. you are the one who got her drunk. they're running the item tomorrow. we're at least going to get some extra press out of this situation. when this tour is over, you are finished. I mean completely finished.

and with that she bolted, slamming the door behind her. great, I thought, she's probably off to the Today Show to rant about how the press is unfair to her daughter. (who, in the meantime, is still in my bed, sleeping and sweating at the same time. pretty. luckily I closed the door to the bedroom before darla could see her.) I leaned against the door, hoping she was gone.

before I could exhale, Darla began pounding on the door again. I could barely open it when her face pushed itself into the crack and hissed, "and if you DARE record another duet with my daughter, if you even think about it, I will personally see to it that you leave the tour and never record music in this town or any other town again in your life. I am darcy's one and only duet partner. NOT you. I am a singer. YOU are a BACKUP DANCER. stay out of the way. do I make myself clear?"

I wanted to spit back "I don't care i hate that stupid song we wrote together! it's a joke! it's almost as bad as yours" but I just nodded and closed the door. she pounded again, yelling, "and get her coat back, pronto!" but I didn't open it. I couldn't take any more. I mean it wasn't even seven a.m.

now tito and probably my mother are going to see darla's story in the papers and they'll think I'm spending the summer lushed out on a cross-country scorpion-bowl tour. ugh.

how did this happen to me? how did I become the fall girl? it was bad enough that they blamed that whole darcy barnes transvestite look-alike contest fiasco on me, now I have to take the heat for darcy's immature liver. I need a latte.

I can't believe it's not even 7 in the morning yet. I'm hung over and I'm horrified.

thank god I'm K.K. right now and not Kelly. I'm not sure I'd be able to deal.

185

To: Tito_T
From: kaykay4real
Date: Friday July 26
Time: 7:05 AM
Subject: Wasn't me
You are still asleep. but I want you to know that no matter what kind of gossip you read online or hear on access Hollywood today, it wasn't me. I love you. help!
K.K.

there was just another knock on the door. it was jesse this time. "Where's darcy?"

she's asleep, I said. goodbye.

he stuck his hand out, blocking the door. "wait, is she asleep? or passed out?"

"what do you think?" I go. now get away.

Passed out? he said. perfect! let me in. he was grinning.

Get . . . the . . . fuck . . . out . . . of . . . here! I screamed, slamming the door and dead bolting it. he banged on the door and yelled "well . . . what are YOU doing? want to hang out?" I ignored him.

If only rashid was here right now. he'd know how to deal. er, actually no he wouldn't. but at least he'd know what to say. sigh. Maybe he wouldn't even know that. but I can't call him anyway. It's 7:10 AM and normal people just aren't up yet.

omigod I just remembered, our new york show is TONIGHT. this is, according to everyone, the big one. Madison Square Garden. it's where Madonna shot her HBO special and everything. anyone willing to add $29.95 to their cable bill will see our show.

and it's my responsibility to drag the star of the show out of her hangover.

I think I'll let her sleep for now. lemme go make sure she's still breathing. I wonder if I have any gum.

RIHGA ROYAL HOTEL, 10:25 AM

Outfit: I dug around and found evan's Insane Clown Posse tee for good luck.
Fortune: Who said life is fair?

---

miraculously I fell back asleep after that encounter with darla. What can I say, life with Regis and Kelly just didn't hold my attention.

but just a couple of minutes ago Eileen called and woke me up.

"ok k.k. I mean Kelly don't talk, just listen. here's the deal. I left the show this morning. I'm sorry this is so sudden but there was no other way around it. darla decided it would be best if I left the tour immediately. I suppose she's right. I mean that's not the kind of press we want to get for darcy. so it's probably best that I go, even though it's not really my fault. it'll make it easier on you all. and I mean why hang around if you're not really wanted right? so here's the scoop. I overheard darla talking on her cell phone . . . I don't know who she was talking to . . . but she was talking about figuring out a way to deal with 'the k.k. issue,' now I'm not sure what the exact k.k. issue is or anything but she said it doesn't sound good. I think you should watch your back for the next little bit. I don't think she would do anything that would mess up the show, so you're probably safe and won't get fired or anything, but this is darla we're talking about so it really could go either way. besides she fired me immediately after realizing I was listening to her conversation so there's that, too. so, um, I'm leaving tonight for LA. sorry I have to miss the big show. hey by the way don dezer gave me the heads-up on a new gig . . . i'm going to manage the FlyGirls2K on the Wayans Brothers' 'Big Pimpin' on UPN Comedy Hour.' want to join the crew when the tour is up? it's a great gig—pretty much how J.Lo got her start you know."

I found myself saying "um, ok" before realizing that actually, no, I don't ever want to be a FlyGirl2K on the new Big Pimpin' Comedy Hour. EVER. oh yeah and remembering that I have much more horrifying things to worry about than ending up a FlyGirl2K. Like Darla.

Eileen could probably tell I didn't know what to say. "ok, ok, I better go. I don't want you getting in trouble for talking to me ok good luck k.k. I mean Kelly. I still have your email address i'll be in touch ok? hang in there be strong and keep up the realness ok?"

oh man, what have I gotten myself into?

To: kaykay4real
From: Tito_T
Date: Friday July 26
Time: 10:05 AM
Subject: Cutie Patootie
You know I only believe what you tell me, sweetie. And you know I'm you're biggest fan. By the way Evan and your

mom are going to come over here to watch your pay-per-view special. He called and asked if he could. How cute is that?
Teet

I was like my MOM is going over to Tito's just to watch me? that's weird.

DINER

NEW YORK CITY, 4:55 PM

Outfit: faded jeans, yellow wifebeater, aviators
Mood: I've never felt like this so I'm not sure what to call it. it's not good, though.

I didn't think things could go from bad to worse until they did.

well actually they got better for a couple of minutes.

I poked my head into the bedroom, saw darcy facedown on the mattress, spread-eagled. no dignity. anyway I thought about checking to see if she was breathing then changed my mind, scrawled a note on a page ripped out of the room service menu (it said "stay in bed, sleepy-head" cause that's what she told me her dad used to say to her on Christmas morning), and stuck the note up to the TV screen. I figured she'd definitely see it there.

then I called rashid's room. "are you up. I need you," I said. he goes, "lobby, 10 minutes."

we met downstairs. we walked over to the hazy, hot concrete plaza in front of the Ziegfeld theater down the block, got iced coffee from the guy selling bagels and stuff there, and grabbed a bench. It was still morning, but it already felt like pea soup outside.

I told him the whole story or at least, all the parts I

knew. he just kept laughing. I was yelling at him, all, this is NOT funny! and everything but he was like the HELL it isn't! this is too funny! I mean, are you kidding me? psycho darla plotting to undermine a backup dancer? calling the newspaper to rant about a BLIND ITEM? it sucks about eileen and everything but come on this is too funny. I was like shut up! it wouldn't be so funny if it was YOU and he goes, "actually, I think laughing at it is the only way I could really handle it" and then he gave me the sweetest biggest hug ever and goes, you can handle it, Kelly. none of this is real. remember that. you, however, *are* real.

I laid my head down in his lap and stared up at him. I felt my keys drop out of my pocket and heard them hit the concrete beneath us.

I go, yeah, it is pretty funny isn't it. and then I started laughing a little. and then laughing harder. and rashid was cracking up right along with me.

Then he stood up and started imitating darla, stroking an imaginary Pekinese and shooting me his rendition of the LOOK. I could barely breathe I was laughing so hard. iced coffee shot out of my nose.

He put his hands around my waist, pulled me toward him, and goes, "your turn."

So I belted out an amazingly accurate, "Do I make myself CLEAR?!" at the top of my lungs. And I started to crack up. But when I looked up at his face to see his reaction, I realized he wasn't looking at me. His face had gone gray and he was looking over my head, behind me.

I turned my head and saw darla standing about 10 yards away, hands on hips, staring. and she had the LOOK on. She walked, slowly, right up to us. Ignoring rashid, she just kept focused on me.

After staring at me for what seemed like an eternity, she goes, "Where is my daughter?"

I didn't say a word. rashid crouched down, reached under the bench, found my room key, and gave it to darla.

she headed back toward the hotel. rashid gave me one last hug, whispered, Let me see if I can chill her out, then chased up 54th Street after darla.

I sat down on the bench and sucked on my iced coffee. I looked at my watch. 11:18 AM. Most days I wouldn't have even been awake yet. But this day is already ruined. I suppose I should have gone up to my room to face darla and make sure darcy was cool. but I didn't. I couldn't. I couldn't picture that tactic working out very well. and I guess I didn't care that much about it either.

besides I knew that I didn't really feel sorry, and apologizing when you don't feel sorry totally sucks.

So I decided to bolt. And wander around the city for hours and hours. At some point it occurred to me that it was my first trip to new york. And that it was exactly the way everyone describes it. Thousands and thousands of people, yet very lonely.

after hours and hours of wandering I went back to the Rihga. unfortunately, everyone (including me, according to the woman cleaning my room) had checked out already (we're supposed to stay somewhere in long island this weekend).

that's why I'm sitting here at this diner. thank god I had $22 on me. and thank god grilled cheese tastes the same no matter where you go.

wow, I'm really broke. what the hell am I going to do about money? I have to get back to the show. I need that check. evan needs it.

ok, it's 5 after 5. I wonder if they're doing sound checks yet?

THE GARDEN

NEW YORK CITY, 7:20 PM

I hate it when big moments in your life, like big ones, get overshadowed by something totally out of your control. it ruins it.

like today, I hailed my very first cab ever in my life. that's a pretty big deal! I stuck out my fist and this cab stopped. but I barely even noticed it because all of a sudden I was so freaked about getting back to the tour. something snapped in that diner and I got this rush of "I've got a job to do!" or something and I knew I had to get to the Garden asap.

(that's what everyone on the tour calls Madison Square Garden. weird huh. like instead of "we're playing in new york" they're all "we're playing at the garden." I had no clue what they were all talking about until, like, yesterday.)

anyway, that was my first cab hailing. turned out I was only like two minutes from the garden.

it took me a while to find the right door because that place is huge. I must have tried like four doors. finally I figured it out. luckily I had my It's Darcy!! i.d. with me. one wave of that sucker and I was in.

as I rode the endless escalators up toward where the security guard told me the dancers' room was, I started to get a little scared. I mean, last I saw darla, she was ready to go house on me and I haven't seen darcy all day and I probably missed sound check. not to mention, it's our biggest show of the tour. I started preparing myself for pretty much anything. have I been fired? did darla lock me out? will darcy totally scream at me? will the dancers freak out at me? will they sabotage me onstage?

will anyone be on my side?

I was prepared to grovel to keep my job. (where else could I make enough for Evan's tuition in just one summer?)

I was ready for my reentry into Darcy land to completely suck. But it didn't.

In fact, the next few hours were totally routine. almost disappointingly so. darla wasn't around anywhere, darcy barely spoke to me except for a "hey do you have any extra body gems" (then again she's always all business before a big show and doesn't want to chitchat, so it's impossible to tell if she's even pissed or anything). our stretching was just like always, although rashid did give me a wink. I tried to smile back but I chickened out. I was staying low.

I started to think that maybe it wasn't a lost cause. maybe I could keep those paychecks coming. after all, that's really why I'm here. isn't it?

but it was strange . . . I know everyone must have heard about what happened (I mean, I disappeared all day.

people notice things like that around here) but no one was acting differently. no one was even trying to avoid me. it was weirder than being ignored . . . it was like no one cared whether *I* was there or not as long as someone was there to dance. it was just like being out on the street earlier today, everyone was too busy thinking about the show to think about me.

it was very x-files. I felt invisible.

Makes sense in a way, I guess. after all, we have the biggest show of the year in like an hour. as long as everyone's here and ready to perform, who cares about what happened today? at least for now.

it's 7:40 now. Nice 'n Easy just finished "Light as a Feather, Stiff as a Board" and ripped off their wicca gowns (they're wearing rainbow-photoprint chaps now with zebra-print bikinis) for "Clue in, Dude." we go on in 20 minutes.

Oh yeah, I just remembered. tito sent me that email that evan was coming over to his place to watch with him . . . And mom.

BACK AT THE RIHGA, 10:56 PM

(this time I'm paying my own way. who knew it was $300 a night? good thing we got paid last week and my atm card still works)

Outfit: I left my It's Darcy!! tour jacket at the garden but I wish I still had it cause the AC is really strong in here and I'm freezing. full show makeup still on. track pants and microweave tee.

Mood: they haven't invented a word for this mood.

To: kaykay4real
From: Tito_T
Date: Friday July 26
Time: 9:05 PM
Subject: Who rules?
You were FABULOUS! You were amazing!
That solo shit you did was incredible!
How come you didn't tell me you had a
solo? Man, your hair is amazing!
Teetow
PS-Your mom came, but she was late and
missed the show. She was really upset.

no surprise there. maybe she was on a date or something.

To: Tito_T
From: kaykay4real
Date: Friday July 26

Time: 10:59 PM

Subject: A list

this has been the most out-of-control
day in my life. Today I

1. woke up hung over. (drank too much
   last night, carried Darcy home from
   her birthday party.)
2. got yelled at at 6:30 AM by Darla,
   pissed that I had "allowed" her
   daughter to make a freakin' specta-
   cle of herself last night (I will
   forward the appropriate gossip item
   shortly)
3. was called a ho by darla, in an
   exclusive interview (you'll see)
4. insulted darla to her face
5. left the tour without telling
   anyone and wandered the streets of
   nyc alone, vowing never to
   return
6. caved and went to do the show
7. was ignored at "the Garden" by everyone in the company
8. tempted fate
9. got a standing ovation
10. got fired
11. had to pay for my own room at this
    fuckin' hotel/motel and it's like 350
    dollars a night but I have no idea
    where else to go

Is there some kind of planetary realign-
ment thing going on? Will it be over
soon? I can't take the stress.
Kelly Kel

ok I should back up a little. where did I leave off? oh yeah, Nice 'n Easy in their I-wanna-be-mariah-really-bad outfits were finishing up.

we sat in the wings until the our beats started, about three minutes later. that announcer guy came on . . . ("ladies and gentlemen, prepare yourself for a journey to a special place, to a world where a boy can be a boy and a girl can be a girl . . .") and we found our spots for the "real" cue, when she goes, "It's Darcy," which is when we basically have to bum rush her and start danc-ing our asses off.

maybe it was the tv cameras, or the extra pressure, or whatever, but . . . the energy was incredible.

everyone was on. everyone was hitting everything, darcy was hitting her notes, the crowd was really into it (I can tell now . . . back around St. Louis I couldn't figure out if they were into it or screaming because that's what they think they're supposed to do . . . but now I can tell when they're screaming because they're really into it). anyway we got through the first section with no hitches at all. I noticed that the sound was the most perfect we've had the whole tour. it was like absolutely everything came together.

we were seriously giving the best concert we'd given all

summer, and it was perfect timing considering we were on TV this time.

second set, perfect section. "Plucky" was the best we'd ever done it, by a lot. I even noticed darla, standing off-stage, watching us with her mouth open like she couldn't believe we were capable of this level. it was the look of someone who all of a sudden realized that what she's created is now too big for her to control.

By the third section I was so psyched we were taping the show for pay-per-view. I knew tito was watching. I knew evan was watching. I knew mom was watching. THAT actually freaked me out for a second and I lost my concentration. but only for a beat.

but I couldn't think about that. there wasn't enough room in my brain. It was the middle of a perfect third set and we were truly KILLING IT in every sense. it was, excuse my French, the best motherfuckin' show ever.

until I let myself go THERE at the exact wrong time.

wait there's someone at my door. it better be that cheeseburger I just ordered.

---

ok it took me like 3 minutes to down that burger. still munching on fries now. they're big, that kind with the skin still on 'em. I love that. really salty. yum. ketchup rules.

Anyway, back to the horror story.

so we're almost through the third section, up to where we do that reggae/dance hall version of "Cellular Love" (currently #3 with a bullet) and I am feeling it. and I start to feel myself going THERE. but for the first time, I feel like I can sort of keep a handle on it. like how rashid was telling me that first dress rehearsal in St. Louis about staying THERE without losing control. I was half floating, half focusing, and I knew I'd never danced better.

then, right after the first chorus (2 verses, 2 choruses, and a bridge to go), darcy's jeans rip. you know, those skintight asymmetrical 80s jeans with the zipper up the ankle . . . in white? anyway they didn't split straight up the back like Jessica Simpson that one time. they split at an angle. this asymmetrical seam that ran across her ass from upper left to lower right totally came apart. Diagonally. Picture it. her waistband and the upper section stayed put, but the bottom half sank. and there was the bottom half of her ass. it reminded me of the grilled cheese sandwich I'd had earlier. cut diagonally. only with a crack.

the thing is, I stayed THERE the whole time. like, I was watching this go on right in front of me, I was faced with darcy's ass (she says she was wearing a nude thong but . . . whatever), I watched her stop dancing and freeze for a second, but I stayed THERE. I kept dancing.

and through the next verse, so did darcy. I gotta say, the girl's a pro. the show must go on or whatever they used to say. doesn't really change the fact that she shook her naked asymmetrical ass (er, make that nude-thonged ass) not only in front of an entire stadium of tweens, but an entire nation gathered in front of their pay-per-view screens. movie stars were watching. other pop stars were watching. her boyfriend was watching. record execs were watching. evan was watching (and how psyched was he?), my mother was watching (oh god). president bush was probably watching. it had to be a truly memorable TV moment. like, you could picture hearing about it on MTV's year-end show and stuff.

but after the second verse, "Baby you know my daddy / Just tell me who's my daddy / Let's take it cellular!" she decided to bolt and change clothes. she patted me on the shoulder on her way off, kinda pushing me toward center stage. it all happened in the crystal-clear haze of being THERE . . . I knew what was happening but my body was so, like, tied to the music, like I was living inside it or something (oh god I'm starting to sound like Debbie Allen) that I didn't give anything too much thought. I just kept pumping. and when she nudged me toward the spotlight, I slowly popped over there.

For a split second I thought no, no, no. this is a bad idea. How many times have I been reminded that this is Darcy's show? How many times have I been reminded not to take center stage, EVER, even in rehearsals when darcy's nowhere to be found?

But the show was suffering right now. Darcy was off-stage. The audience had nothing to focus on. And darcy definitely pushed me into the spotlight. She WANTED me to take over.

and I went for it. all of a sudden I was improvising my way through the bridge (one of the backup vocalists took over darcy's singing part . . . if I'd had a mike I'd probably have done the same thing) and the crowd started heating up even more. punch, punch, rebound . . . I was really pulling moves from I don't know where. all I could see was the spotlight, all I could hear was the crowd. louder, louder.

the bridge ran out and it was into the final chorus, which I know perfectly well repeats three times into a fadeout, when we leave the stage to change for the encore. but instead of winding down, I was turning it up. the screams were like pushing me over the top. I just didn't want the moment to end. three reps of the chorus turned into four and then five. I stayed THERE. the crowd continued to cheer, so I kept at it.

I knew I was on dangerous ground, but I didn't know how to get out of it at this point.

until I caught a glimpse of rashid, which pulled me out of the whole thing. he wasn't smiling. he was looking at me like CHILL! I noticed that all the other dancers had stuck to the program and had long since left the stage. but the crowd was chanting, "Go backup! Go backup!" like, "Go ricki Go ricki" and I heard another chorus winding up, so I tried to keep dancing.

but it wasn't the same. I wasn't THERE anymore. I looked back at rashid. he'd turned away. then I saw D-Run, Armand, and Tina staring at me.

then I saw darcy, standing there in new white jeans with her mouth open like somewhere between "wow! Thanks for saving my ass" and "you are amazing!" and "you bitch I hate you," like somewhere between those fans out there and the darcy barnes darla wants her to be.

then I saw darla, offstage, with that LOOK on. turned up to volume 10. like THE LOOK.

I stumbled through a couple more bars, then headed straight offstage, straight to the dressing area to change for "Love You Like a Lollipop" (our first encore). the crowd was going crizazy, still chanting, "GO BACKUP! GO BACKUP!" we only have 60 seconds to change so no one had any time to say anything, but I could feel darla and the LOOK burning into me the whole time.

I kept it together on the outside, but inside I was completely freaking out, feeling really conspicuous and totally on autopilot. I think something inside me knew that I just had to let my body finish out the show and not think. it was my only option. besides I was sure I'd be fired. maybe all that disaster-prep thought from this afternoon would come in handy after all.

but seriously, don't watch me while I change. it's really humiliating being glared at like when you're butt naked, bending over, changing your bra, trying to squeegee yourself into a harlequin bodysuit. it was like she was staring at me coming up with really insidious ways to get me back.

I didn't even give myself the pleasure of thinking or saying "but I only did what darcy wanted . . . I mean the show must go on right" because I mean this is *darla*, it's not like I can argue with her. I'm sure she thinks I planned on stealing my own moment in her baby's show. whatever I can't deal. obviously I'm screwed so what's the point.

the encore went smoothly enough, everyone hit everything all right, but the entire crew was distracted. I was sooo happy when the encores were over. I bolted straight for the dressing room. I wanted to be out of there and back to the hotel before darla got back from tonight's "Mama Knows Best" moment. I figured if I could put some more time between now and when darla confronts me, maybe she'll chill a little. I started scrambling to get out of my bodysuit, and I even accidentally tore it under the arm. (damn, did I just do that?) I threw on my It's Darcy!! tour jacket and headed for the door. that's when I realized I didn't know where I was going. I forgot we were changing hotels tonight. I hesitated for a moment, and darla burst in, stroking that freakin' dog in that freakin' purse.

Oh man, here it comes.

she goes, How dare you? HOW DARE YOU? How dare you conspire to steal my show . . . I mean my daughter's show . . . directly out from underneath her? In front of an exclusive pay-per-view audience? who do you think you are? Don't think I don't know about your whole little master plan to take my place . . . I mean my daughter's place! Shhh! Punkin! she hissed at the dog.

I was like what is she TALKING about? a master plan? the last thing I want to be is her daughter! but I didn't say anything because darla was still talking:

Then the joyriding in the navigator. The side-by-side tanning. The masquerading with Jesse. The DUET! (I'm like damn I didn't realize I was so conniving, stop touching your dog like that it's gross.)

darla was still going at it. "and then you move in and steal what could be her biggest hit ever."

(oddly, when she said that all I could think was I seriously don't know that "Cellular Love" is going to be that big. I mean, it's just not "Now That's What I Call Music" material. but whatever.)

Then she goes below the belt, in true darla style. she goes, Have you simply not realized where you belong? I hear people say that you're so real, and you think it's a compliment. But don't you see that "real" is just a nice way of saying you're "average"? Don't you get it? You have no special talent. you have a skill that any monkey could learn. sure, people tell you that you're real. They never say you're *special*.

I was like OUCH!

she goes, Perhaps I haven't made myself clear. You will NEVER be the star. Understand?

because as of right now, you are fired. do you understand? unemployed. unwelcome. darcy and I both agree that not only are you not up to the level of talent and commitment that this show needs, but you are actually poisonous to the company. you are a virus, K.K. or whatever your real name is. Give me your pass. I was like I have a contract and she goes, Don't make this worse because I can destroy you in this business.

I'm kinda like whatever, and she goes, You'll never dance again if I have anything to say about it. she was getting really soap opera-y. I rolled my eyes.

but then she goes, hissing, Watch your step, Kimball. Leave quietly and forget your contract. I can ruin everything for you. *Everything.* I can ruin your life. Not to mention Evan's.

that's all she needed to say. she threatens to mess with Evan? I'm out of there. I have no idea what she knows about evan or anything, but evan is one thing I am NOT willing to risk.

a second cab-hailing and I'm back at the rihga, $300-plus poorer.

From the New York City Times-Herald Daily News

You figure it out . . .

. . . Which teenage trollop, so wiped out after a wildly successful on-air concert, reportedly collapsed into the arms of her equally limelight-friendly (but incognito, don't you know) paramour après-gig, promising to spend the next three days hotel room–bound, ordering fried chicken and barbecue chips and watching public access TV? Hint: She also mentioned a craving for an unmentionable substance that might cause a champion munchie fest such as just described. Sources say her exhaustion was more than physical, citing "extensive backstage drama and tension," so perhaps the herbal Rx is just what this girl wants.

So jesse was in town after all. Pothead.

TITO'S HOUSE, 7:30 AM (I'm still on east coast time I think)

Outfit: tito's zebra-print boxer shorts and nothing else. It's ok, tito's already seen my boobs.

Hair: tito freaked out at how damaged it is. he's gonna see if he has any deep-conditioning hair mask thingies later.

Mood: that kinda tired where you think you could happily spend four days in bed watching tv. or maybe four weeks.

Fortune: There's no place like home. (I freaked out when I read this. I was like YEAH!! except I'm not at home. I'm at tito's. which I guess feels more like home these days than carl's and mom's. not that I would know since I haven't been there yet. I'd feel bad except I know evan's away on that complimentary one-week nature-camp thing in utah someplace sponsored by the local sheriff's department with the other kids in his school so there's no reason for me to visit home.)

I don't know how I managed it, but I made it home to San Diego last night at like midnight. without even so much as a goodbye from D-run, armand, or jesus. not even rashid said goodbye. I left him three messages, but then I was out the door. I wonder why I didn't hear back from him.

it was a pretty lonely plane ride. I was stuck in between a dutch backpacker who needed a shower and a woman who asked me at least three times whether I'd accepted Jesus Christ as my personal lord and savior. luckily I had my discman.

anyway I took a cab straight from the airport right to tito's place—his messy, wonderful place. I crashed here last night. His mother doesn't know I'm here yet. we might not tell her.

what can I say I just didn't want to go home right away. I didn't know what it would be like, and right now I need to chill. plus I need to figure out what to do about money. I'm not sure what I'm going to come out with. I mean, I definitely won't get paid through my contract, so anything I have now is pretty much all I've got.

and it's nowhere near enough for the martino school.

I don't know what I'm going to do. we need that cash.

thank god for tito. he's over there snoring. I'm wide awake and he's snoring. it just doesn't seem right that tito would snore but he does. really loudly. but I love him. he didn't once ask "what are you going to do about the money" even though I know he was wondering about it.

it's kinda nice to be able to think about things like that for a change. I am so sick of watching my ass. I am so sick of watching darcy's ass. I am so sick of that quote-unquote pop star life.

I think.

TITO'S HOUSE, 4 PM

Outfit: still in tito's boxer shorts. I actually haven't left the house in two days. just watching tons of tv and eating Popsicles. it's exactly what I've been needing.
Hair: tito cut off like three inches last night. no more split ends thank god.
Mood: in hiding and loving it

They talked about me on MTV news last night. he was at the darcy barnes show and did this whole backstage thing (which I never even noticed them filming when I was there but whatever there are always so many people around those things) but when he was talking about the concert he was like blah blah darcy looked great and everything and blah blah but then he goes, "New York City and pay-per-view fans got an extra treat most tour attendees will miss this season when a gracious Darcy Barnes turned over the stage to breakout backup dancer K.K. Kimball for several minutes during Friday's show at the famed Madison Square Garden. While the concert was already an amazing event that didn't need any help from anyone, K.K. took things to a different level, bringing a sense of realness to the arena and proving herself to be headed for certain solo stardom one day. For her part, Darcy proved herself to be a class act by showcasing one of the other talented dancers in her show. It's the mark of a great star, and the audience was crazy for it."

I was like TURN that off! and he switched to E! and there was some gossip columnist talking about me all "she's the latest scene-stealer on the teen circuit, and she's au natural up top! stay tuned . . ." I was like omigod and he switched to Entertainment Tonight and there was some reporter talking about me, then on Extra there was another reporter who looked exactly like the last one, talking about me. then he switched back to MTV and this random chick came on camera with her name and age across the bottom of the screen: Andrea Boone, 14: "When that one dancer was up there, like, THAT was the best part of the show!" and then this other kid said the same thing. and then another one said it and her three friends all went "WOOOOOHOOOO!" all TRL style. tito and I looked at each other like no WAY! you got the TRL scream! he goes, "I have to go get out your chart, right away. You are going through WAY too much transition right now!"

turns out my chart says there's nothing special going on. guess this is just my life.

I was like what about money? what's it say about money?

he goes, Not so good. you better get off the couch and get back to work pretty soon.

I sank my head. how could I have blown such a sweet job.

the weirdest thing was, when we were watching tv, it

213

really didn't feel like all those people on TV were talking about ME. even though it was only a couple of
days ago, I feel like it was a thousand years ago and it
happened to someone else. only it didn't. it happened
to me.

TITO'S, 5:30 PM

Fortune: Luck can strike twice. Good *or* bad.

I never thought it was over, that it was all over and I'd go back to my normal life. that is, until I checked my email at tito's:

To: Kel_Kimball
From: EileenW_hitpatrol
Date: Monday July 29
Time: 5:16 AM
Subject: Another gig, $$$
I heard about everything. I'm not sure where you are right now, but I hope you get this. Here's the deal. I just got off the phone with Pashmina's people. Did you know that Shania, the girl you replaced in the Darcy show, ended up going to Pashmina's show? It was OK with her injury and all because they don't dance as hard over there. But anyway Shania's leaving the tour again, this time because she hooked up with Pashmina's manager, who Pashmina was supposedly dating or something; anyway, they're both totally fired. And you thought the drama was serious over at Darcy Live!! Anyway, there are still

five weeks left on the "Pashmina with Love" tour and she saw Darcy's pay-per-view show and she heard about what happened afterward, and I told her how real you really are, and long story short she wants you to join her tour . . . so can you be in Chicago by Tuesday? Plenty of $$—more than you were getting I think plus the Pop-Tarts are opening how funny is that? I know the Pashmina doll doesn't sell as well as the Darcy one (ha ha) but please call me on my cell as soon as you can.

oh man, here we go again. I figure, what the hell?

I hope tito was right when he told me to go for it. i mean, i knew I would, i guess. but I was still like DUDE I need to get OUT of that craziness don't you think and he was like, "um, NO you dipshit it's what you've always wanted to do and besides it's only for the summer and you know I need you out there getting details."

so I was like yeah but look what they're saying about me on tv! and he was like "are *they* paying evan's tuition? you're going."

yeah, he was right. what the hell, right?

BACKSTAGE AT THE CHICAGO CENTER, 7:45 PM (was just here a month ago with darcy. the security guard remembered me. ha ha.)

Outfit: they're making me wear a grass green bodysuit with a diamond cut out of the middle so you see my belly button and what I like to call my under-cleavage. it's bejeweled all around the cut. I have glitter in my hair and jewels running down my part. I have so much makeup on I smell like a drag queen. Tito would be proud or horrified. I'm not sure which.
Fortune: Trust your instinct.

Tito just sent me this gossip item online:

From the **New York Morning Star Herald-Tribune Post**

Just asking . . .

. . . Which princess of pop, recently voted among the ten sexiest women in the world by a major British young men's magazine, is less than confident about her natural beauty? Seems this divette spends nearly 7 hours in the makeup chair before any photos are allowed! One editor on a recent cover shoot for a glossy teenybopper magazine complained, "By the time Miss Thing was happy with her makeup, the sun had set. We had to cancel the shoot."

He sure knows how to make me feel better when I'm nervous.

we go on in a half hour in front of 20,000 people. again.
I "learned" the whole show today, in one day, but i've
never done it all the way through. and I haven't even
met Pashmina yet.

CHICAGO HOTEL, 11:30 PM

Outfit: cloud pjs and black tank
Mood: relief

---

whew.

I just got back to the room. the show went all right. I stayed in the back and just followed everyone else. luckily it wasn't that much for me . . . the guys dance a lot more than the girls in this show, mostly with their shirts off, which could be hot but it isn't. most of us girls just writhe around and stuff. I would say it's about ¼ as much dancing as in Darcy's show . . . here we're pretty much just strippers who keep their clothes on. also Pashmina obviously does a lot of slow songs too so when you break it down there isn't all that much dancing to do.

anyway I didn't screw up too bad. I just decided I would pretend it was like a rehearsal and just get everything right. I barely even noticed the crowd or anything like that. hey, I'd already seen enough crowds before, right? funny that sometimes the crowd can be like RIGHT THERE in your face and other times it's like wallpaper in the background. tonight it was wallpaper.

anyway I was really trying not to fuck up, so I just paid attention to the other dancers and everything especially this one named Elena who's really good. I mean, she's

219

not that good but her moves are really exaggerated and easy to follow and stuff. I mean, she IS good, but you know what I mean. whatever.

so meanwhile, even though I've danced behind her and even writhed around her leg once, I still haven't really met Pashmina. well, sort of but not really. like after the whole entire show was over she came up to me with Bernie her big bodyguard dude and looked at me with this face packed FULL of makeup and gloss and glitter and shine and laminate and pencil and liner and lipstick and these lashes that actually made me want to stand back a couple of paces and she goes, "you're K.K. right? I've heard about you. I'm not sure your outfit was working right tonight. see if they can refit you?"

I was about to go "it's Kelly, actually" but Pashmina was already gone. so it's gonna be like that. guess this diva isn't looking for a best friend.

I wonder if she thinks I'm fat, like darla?

SlipKnotRules933111: dude whatsup

KellyKelSoCal321: so much. you wouldn't believe it. how was boot camp? how's life without the twins

SlipKnotRules933111: actually I kind of miss them there's not enough to hate around here at the moment. except just being here. Nature camp (not boot camp! Jeez!) was pretty cool. they kicked our asses but it was awesome being out there. we even saw a forest fire. I want to be a fire ranger now.

KellyKelSoCal321: no WAY! that is so COOL!

SlipKnotRules933111: have you seen that show More True Fire Ranger Disasters?

KellyKelSoCal321: no. should I?

SlipKnotRules933111: yes. it rules.

KellyKelSoCal321: when is it on

SlipKnotRules933111: I forget. say hi to darcy for me

KellyKelSoCal321: I can't dude I don't work for her anymore. I'm in Chicago with Pashmina.

SlipKnotRules933111: huh? Pashmina who? I think that show's on wednesday now that I think about it but it might be Thursday

KellyKelSoCal321: evan pay attention. I just found out we're playing in san diego in a couple of days.

SlipKnotRules933111: you and darcy are coming to san diego?

KellyKelSoCal321: no, Pashmina

SlipKnotRules933111: huh?

KellyKelSoCal321: forget it. good night evan.

yeah it's true. we're playing the Junior Miss Teen United States pageant or something in San Diego sunday night. I have to tell tito! he can make sure evan and mom come to the show.

THE BUS, 11:30 PM

Outfit: Pashmina with Love windbreaker, cutoff skate shorts.
Fortune: Steady as she goes.

To: Tito_T
From: kaykay4real
Date: Thursday August 1
Time: 11:31 PM
Subject: The Pashmina Scene
First of all Pashmina's bus is way nicer than Darcy's. she has a steam shower and a king-size bed and two tvs and two refrigerators. half the bus is her closet and dressing room. it's all animal prints and mirrors. mirrors everywhere actually. except I don't get to ride on it. only hector her, um, "boyfriend" gets to stay on that one, at least when Pashmina's not "hanging out" with another guy or something. or when hector is. last night we pulled over in the middle of the night so he could get off our bus and onto her bus. hector's kinda like Pashmina's fake boyfriend. except, um, how do I say this . . . hector's not really into any of the girls here. he's into the boys. at least I think so. I

mean, all the boys seem to be into each
other. in fact, everyone seems to be
into everyone else here and I can't figure out what's going on. plus everyone
bolts right after the show to go out to
gay bars. even the girls go to the gay
bars. I guess it's because the music is
better or something.
Second of all Pashmina's dancers aren't
any nicer than darcy's. I think that whole
thing about dancers all being best friends
and everything is a big load. there are
total cliques and everyone's competitive
and harsh on each other and everything
else. not to mention someone already stole
my All-American rejects cd. or else I lost
it. but I think someone stole it.
third of all Pashmina isn't the nicest
kid on the block. well it's not so much
that. it's just that all she does is
work I guess and doesn't hang that much.
and when she does hang she just talks
about herself. I feel bad for her she
seems really really exhausted. and everyone thinks she's so skanky.
I mean, I know I thought she was a skank
before, but now I don't know. she's a
strange one, but she's kinda scared of her
own shadow. and she's no more skanky than
half the girls we know at school. ok she

wears way skankier outfits, especially
onstage, and that's pretty nasty, but
she's not like screwing every guy in sight
to try and get them to like her.
I guess she seems lonely or something.
then again that might have to do with the
fact that she can be such a raving BIOTCH.
Especially when she doesn't get her Arby's
Beef 'n Cheddar Deluxe and Mr. Pibb.
anyway I've pretty much got the dances
down for this show. but to be honest
with you I'm not trying that hard. the
dances aren't that complex, and my heart
isn't in it. maybe it's these clothes.
have you seen how tacky they are?
but like I say the dances are way easy
compared to darcy's. and no one's there
to see them anyway. they come to hear
her SING, actually sing. and I gotta
tell you her voice is really amazing.
say whatever you want about her but that
girl can WAIL! LOUD! and long! she is
all about hitting those big huge notes
and hanging on to them for like ever.
the audience FREAKS! and it's weird
because she's soooo small. like a size
zero. except for her hair. if you can
call it hers. ha ha.
I guess when you're that small you feel
like you gotta dress, like, harder or

something. like this girl dresses like a
straight-up HO sometimes. (voulez vous
couchez avec moi?) she's always making the
stylists and everyone give her smaller,
sexier, sluttier clothes. you'd think it
would be all her handlers and whatever who
are really pushing her that way . . . but
the truth is she'd be in hot shorts and
pasties if it were up to her. There's something really cool about it though . . .
it's like she's doing what she wants, you
know? or more to the point, doing what
sells. and say what you want, the girl is
banking, fo' rizzle.
no annoying stage mothers, at least not
as far as I can tell. in fact, there's
hardly any evidence of Pashmina's family
at all. I think her parents were divorced
and Pashmina grew up with her dad. I'm
not sure what the story is with her mom,
someone told me they barely know each
other. people always whisper when they
talk about Pashmina's past. like it was a
rough childhood or something.
there are all these industry people lin-
gering around. They act like they want to
be in the sopranos or something. like,
total wannabe mobsters. some of them are
cute. but they freak me out. it's like
the men in black but kinda rougher. and

the thing is everyone seems really scared
of Pashmina. like, the men in black at
It's Darcy!! were focused on being really
protective of darcy. the crew at Pashmina
with Love are more focused on not pissing
her off. know what I mean.
oh yeah and there's this whole contin-
gent of department store queens flitter-
ing around her all the time spritzing
her with essential oils and stuff. oh,
did I mention Pashmina has a new cosmetics line called Wet.
the choreographer, Jilly, has been working
me out pretty hard, but it's cool I
guess. I need to know the dances, right?
and I know I need the money from this
gig. look at me all "gig" like I'm a show
business pro now. that's me, Kelly
Kimball, rock star. whatever. anyway I get
no free time and neither does Jilly until
I know everything. you can imagine how
psyched jilly is about that. whatever,
she's pretty cool. very intense. no jokes.
I even tried to bust on darcy and
Pashmina's piercings and she wouldn't bite
at all. not even a smile. but she's a
good teacher. she moves fast, like I do.
so am I having fun? I don't know. they're
totally keeping me away from the press,
which is good, because I heard that all

these darcy fans are HATING me right now
or something and I really wouldn't know
what to say about it anyway. like anyone
has any clue what happened. freaks. but
it is really really weird to know that
all these people are like putting up web-
sites about you, well not really about
you because they don't know you and they
get the story messed up, all saying how
much they hate you and everything it's
crazy. like, could they please get a
life? but it's like you can't fight back
because you don't even know who to talk
to. so whatever I'm just going from van
to hotel to bus to van to venue to hotel
to van to studio to wherever.
it's cool since we're going to all the
cities I've already been to this summer.
the last show is in St. Louis, you know,
Pashmina's hometown. it's not so good for
my tan, though, being inside all the time,
and Pashmina's not feeling the whole side-
by-side tanning session vibe. (what can I
say I got used to having a natural glow!)
she seems pretty, like, *hard* if you ask
me. like, darcy seems like this showbiz
kid who was kept young. Pashmina is this
showbiz kid who was an adult before her
time. there's a real difference, know
what I'm saying?

oh yeah and I'm riding on the dancers'
bus. in a bunk. a bottom bunk. under
tywan. yes, that's his name. he's from
Vancouver. (so far I've counted five
buses. one of them got broken into in
june so they're all bulletproof now.)
did I mention that for her second encore
she sings, um, "Papa Can You Hear Me" by
Barbra Streisand? it's too weird.
no confirmation on any piercings. yet.
but you know I'll be keeping you posted.
information appears to be forthcoming as
Pashmina seems prone to dressing in zip-
up hoodies with nothing underneath. Ew!
xo
Kel

INDIANAPOLIS (I THINK), 3:36 PM

Hair: have you ever tried to wash your hair on the bus?
Fortune: Some days are better than others. Some aren't.

Pashmina handed this to me this morning in my hotel room:

SOUR GRAPES MAKE SOUR WINE

. . . Seems Darla Barnes, beloved mama-san of teen pop queen Darcy Barnes, has become more than just a nuisance to her baby girl's biggest chart and tour rival, Pashmina and is threatening to sue the competing camp for creative copyright infringement. The meddling matriarch claims that when "Pashmina with Love" hired a backup dancer who'd just left "It's Darcy," the choreography took on more than just an incidental resemblance to Darcy's.

Experts say Darla has no case, but it certainly adds more fuel to the "copycat" fire, which Pashmina especially despises. Insiders speculate Darla's bizarre behavior could be sour grapes—after all, Pashmina's show is the one that truly proved the pundits wrong and sold stronger than all predictions. $42 mil and counting, thank you very much.

oh man, I thought. I'm nowhere near Darla and she's still talking about me.

Pashmina goes, all hard, This Darla woman. Can you turn her off?

I go, I wish I could, I'm sorry, I can't believe this.

she goes, We don't need these bad vibes here k.k. see what you can do about it.

I was like ok, I sure will. Pashmina turned around and left.

what could *I* possibly do about darla? nothing. and Pashmina was right . . . there are some real bad vibes following me around right now. but I don't know what to do about it. bitch.

I crawled onto the middle of my king-size bed and closed my eyes. all I want to do here is dance.

I sat there, cross-legged, with my head in my hands. I wanted to call someone, but I didn't know who to call. tito? evan? rashid? mom? would anyone understand?

I let my mind wander over my ever-more-confusing sitch and realized I'd started to hum. I closed my eyes and swayed back and forth slowly, imagining dad with a guitar, singing to me.

"All the leaves are brown / and the sky is gray . . ."

soon I was singing along with dad in my head, then I realized I was singing for real. eyes still closed, I started to turn up the volume. "Caaaalifornia dreamin' . . ."

soon I was standing on the bed, belting out the melody. I guess I figured if I sang loud enough, I'd be able to block out all the other noise . . . darla, Pashmina, darcy, evan . . .

as I came off the second chorus, I realized I was hearing a harmony against my melody, and for a split second I was like wow I have a great voice! but then I realized I wasn't alone.

I opened my eyes and there stood Pashmina, singing with me, with a big ol' smile on her face.

I clamped my mouth shut. "hi" she goes. Hey I heard you out in the hallway and your door was open. you're good. your voice is good with mine. she goes I need to figure out how to deal with the harmony in the bridge of "Girls Want It, Part 2" for when we do it at the pageant in San Diego. do me a favor, sing this . . .

she hummed a phrase, I mimicked her.

she goes, ok, again. this time I'll come in with a harmony.

I did, and she did, and it sounded amazing. she had a big grin on her face.

Wow, she goes. That sounds good.

our eyes connected. there's something about harmonizing with someone. it's like your voice and their voice make a totally new voice that doesn't belong to either one of you. very cool.

we locked eyes and did it one more time. was she really going to ask me to sing with her in san diego? I felt like I was off the hook for that whole darla situation.

suddenly her grin left her face. You're good, she said, But I think I'll sing along to a track of myself on Sunday. anyway, see you later at the show. and she left.

um, ok.

KellyKelSoCal321: I got tickets for you and mom

SlipKnotRules933111: for what

KellyKelSoCal321: for the show in san diego on Sunday.

SlipKnotRules933111: what about tito?

KellyKelSoCal321: yeah him too. :-) that's cute you thought of him.

KellyKelSoCal321: I'm not sure where the show is you have to look it up online ok? can you remember? sunday night. the tickets will be at the box office or whatever waiting for you. I'll email more info.

SlipKnotRules933111: k

KellyKelSoCal321: got all that?

KellyKelSoCal321: got all that?

SlipKnotRules933111: I'm not an idiot

KellyKelSoCal321: no you're just a delinquent

SlipKnotRules933111: ha ha

KellyKelSoCal321: I'll make sure u get passes backstage too. don't forget to come back after the show. and don't forget to tell tito, ok?

GRAND HOTEL

SAN DIEGO, 11:11 PM

(it is so weird to be in my hometown and be staying in a hotel.)

Outfit: black t-shirt bedazzled with 666 across the front.

Mood: big pimpin' in san diego. yeah, right.

---

the Miss Teen United States show—we performed during the swimsuit competition—was sort of a bust. the acoustics SUCKED and everyone was off tempo. it was almost embarrassing. still Pashmina managed to pull out her voice and improvise and totally saved the show so we weren't humiliated. in fact she came off looking brilliant. it was just the rest of us who bit. ugh whatever, I heard she has a heavy flow, so there. (I can be so juvenile in my head. love it.)

after the show I was hanging out backstage, changing, kind of watching out for evan and tito and mom. I changed my clothes, took off my makeup, washed my hands, put an avocado/jojoba/ragweed conditioner in my hair (I wanted to make tito proud), even read a couple of magazines waiting for them. the other dancers started to pack up and leave. pretty soon there was hardly anyone left around.

I read another magazine. there was this huge article with darcy barnes in it. she seriously goes, "It is so hard to keep friends in this business. You never know when people will turn on you." I was like ugh whatEVER.

still no evan or tito or mom. where is everyone?! I was about to call tito's mom (which he FORBIDS me to do) to find out what's up when I hear tito screaming: "HEY DIVA!!"

I spun around and saw them walking toward me. I ran in their direction. I was like, "Hi omigod it's sooo good to see you . . . yay you made it to the show!! I know I know the show totally sucked, I'm sorry . . ."

no one said anything.

then mom goes, baby it's so good to see you I miss you there's so much going on oh you look so great honey! and I'm so sorry blah blah.

I'm like sorry for what.

and she goes, "oh sweetie don't you know we missed the show tonight. we thought it was starting later. I guess they tape it earlier than they show it or some-thing I don't know but we got here and the show's over and I guess we had the wrong information."

my shoulders slumped. I was like you missed the show?

all three of them nodded in unison.

tito was like "we're sorry."

I dropped my head. It's ok, I said.

I guess I was used to mom missing my shows.

actually, no I wasn't. I was pretty pissed but I kept quiet while mom kept talking

she goes, I'm so sorry baby. I love you so much. there's just so much going on. carl is gone. we have to move in like the next 2 weeks. I just don't know how we're going to afford our own place. and evan's school. Carl's moving to LA, which is good because we can't leave san diego and I've been temping and I'm applying to get back into teaching in the fall but it's probably only going to be substitute for a year and I can't believe I quit working to take care of that man's kids I mean there were times that he really scared me, but . . . sweetie look at your hair it's so cute and you look great I missed you so much. I don't know what happened sweetie. I just got lost. I just didn't want a second marriage to go bad. I know it's not my fault, I don't know. I don't know. I'm sorry. I know you didn't get along with them. honey look how skinny you are I miss you. what are we going to do about evan and his school?

I mumbled about how I had some money put aside for evan, about how this summer I'd saved almost $4,000 for his tuition.

evan wandered off right then. tito goes, "wow that's a lot."

mom said no, you keep that. that won't help. then she said that was about $12,000 short for the year. she said the twelve-thousand-dollars part really slow. it was like she was announcing it to an audience or something. That won't help, she said. she started to sniffle.

I was seething. not only could she not make it to my show to see me dance, she can't even appreciate what I'm doing for evan. I wasn't sure if I was more mad at myself or at her.

mom, you know what? thanks for missing my show. I'll let you know when I'm back in town. tito, evan, later. I turned and walked out. forget this, I thought.

on my way out the door I walked past Pashmina's dressing room. the door was ajar, and I could see her there, alone, staring into the mirror and pulling off her fake eyelashes. she looked even lonelier than I was. she looked at me in the mirror, then looked back at herself. I left.

I went back to the hotel by myself. there I had the most beautiful view of the san diego harbor. this was my hometown, and I was atop it. all by myself.

so this is what success feels like, I thought.

there's someone at the door. hold on.

GRAND HOTEL

SAN DIEGO, 11:55 PM

That was Pashmina at the door.

Her hair was tied back in a ponytail, she had no makeup at all on, and she was wearing nothing but one of the hotel's brown terry robes. it swallowed her up. I was amazed at how different she looked out of costume. she was small, with big eyes. she looked like ET. (but a lot prettier, if she's reading this.) anyway she goes, "hi" and her voice was really really soft, kinda shaky and nervous.

I go, Hi.

she goes, Listen I don't want to make a big deal out of this but I overheard you and your mom talking in the dancers' dressing room earlier and I just want you to know I know what you're going through and she hands me an envelope. "I know what it's like when your family is all crazy like that. this is for your brother. don't thank me, and do me a favor and let's not talk about this again.

and she left. she was there only like 30 seconds and never really looked me in the eyes the whole time. she came and went so fast I wasn't sure she had actually been there. I didn't know what just happened.

237

then I remembered the envelope in my hand. I opened it up and found two checks . . . one from "Pashmina with Love, Inc." for $10,000 and one from her personal checking account for $2,000. $12,000 altogether.

I was pretty stunned. but all I could think about was how mean I was to my mom tonight.

ON THE BUS

JUST LEFT MIDLAND, TX, 11 PM

Outfit: Don't laugh . . . cowboy hat. what can I say I look pretty good in it.
Hair: ok, ok, I have braids in too. I know, I know.
Mood: Oddly relaxed.

I haven't written much, haven't had time. we've done 6 shows a week, and my days off I was in a coma. was I just in San Diego?

but we're in the home stretch.

I haven't spoken to mom, but I managed to get tito on the phone for a couple of minutes on Tuesday night I think it was. he said he'd seen my mom a few times since I was in san diego and that she's doing ok. I was like tito you're the best. and he is.

I told him about the money. he was amazed. I told him not to tell anyone but I bet he'll tell my mom.

this tour is way different than darcy's. people keep their heads down here. I was the only one who cracked up when we were watching TV on the bus and there was this shot of Pashmina saying "I'd love to go to the Monte Carlo Music Awards. Where are they being held this year?" everyone was like too scared to giggle or anything. it was weird. you would have thought people could find some comedy there.

also with darcy I never had to, like, wait for the bathroom on the bus or anything . . . I was riding with darcy. this time I'm with seven other dancers and four band guys (the rest of the band has another bus. yep, she travels with a full band . . .) so it's really interesting when we crash at night. er, try to crash at night. it's not like everyone's making out with everyone else. but of course there's one couple on the tour, the d-run and tina if you will, and they're noisier by the night. then there's the basic "we're all sleeping in the same place" giggling or fighting or farting or whatever. it's like no sleep till we get where we're going. it's not exactly a *playful* group, just a busy one.

the only sucky thing is Pashmina hasn't even really let me say "thanks" or anything for the money she gave me. I mean, I went to my bank first thing the next morning (good thing I was in san diego) and opened up a new account so it could earn some interest before evan's tuition was due.

anyway so evan doesn't have to worry but every time I've tried to corner Pashmina to thank her she's been really cold, like "I can't talk now." once she even said "don't worry it was tax-free and I can write it off" so I just scribbled her a thank-you card and gave it to her bodyguard and gave up. and I never heard another word about it.

I found out later that she's actually opening a career center for recently released juvenile delinquents in her hometown. which I have to say is pretty cool.

STILL ON THE BUS, 12:30 AM

---

something came over the radio like 20 minutes ago . . . there are reports that darcy barnes and jesse nixon were killed in a car crash.

I'm worried. I guess I do care after all.

I've been trying to page darcy but getting no response. damn I don't even know if I have the right number.

I borrowed the bassist's satellite modem hookup and emailed her, too. he wouldn't let me surf for news, though . . . he said his battery's been running out too fast lately and he needs to save energy so he can email his daughter in the morning.

also he said it'll just make us all more freaked out because we'll find conflicting information and no one knows the real story yet so why make yourself more crazy by surfing around when you won't find anything any faster than the people at the radio station? why not wait for the official news?

I was like whatever. that's my *friend.* I just pulled on my headphones and turned up my Dido CD and stared out the window watching the headlights racing by.

HOUSTON RITZ

HOUSTON, 11 PM

Outfit: still in the cowboy hat but have big fat sunglasses now. didn't sleep much last night was just worried about darcy. I mean she's my friend even though we left on really bad terms and everything. anyway we found out this morning at 3 AM that it was definitely not true . . . actually they were together at hogs 'n heifers all night.
Mood: Cranky. see not sleeping comment above.
Fortune: it's true . . . things happen in threes.

I was so relieved that darcy wasn't dead.

but we got some even more important news this morning when we pulled into the hotel in Houston.

Pashmina was shoveling down a little tub of Kozy Shack when she climbed onto our bus before anyone could get off and goes, "ok we're postponing our Mobile and Birmingham shows this coming week because we're going to new york to be on the new divas alive. I'll be flying on wednesday, the rest of you will drive up leaving monday. we begin rehearsals on Wednesday night."

at first I was like omigod am I gonna meet gwen stefani or faith or maybe mariah? am I at least gonna meet Gloria Estefan? she's always at those things!

then I was like probably not. we'll all be shoved into the

tackiest back greenroom as usual. backup dancers are always like totally ignored by everyone else. kinda like opening acts.

then it hit me. oh no. OH NO! that means everyone's going to be in the same room together. everyone. Me. Darcy, who could hate me as far as I know . . . and I don't know for sure, not having spoken to her since . . . you know. Pashmina. Darla who will not leave me alone no matter what I do. Jesse who probably has crabs. Rashid who will know what to say if I manage to score a second with him. Jesus, Armand, D-Run, the Tinas who will all ignore me. maybe the elusive, accident-prone Shania will make an appearance. who the hell knows?

is this good news? or bad news? or just a reminder that the drama really *doesn't* stop?

anyway, so then I was flipping through the TV and came across an episode of oprah.

it was all about mothers and daughters and I know you don't have to think too hard to know who were the featured celeb guests. Darcy and Darla.

Oprah said that according to a recent poll, darcy is considered "inspiring" by more people than God.

There was mad tension between them. I mean when they sang "Mama Knows Best" they were both like clenching their jaws and everything. usually darcy's got the whole smiley kitty-cat eyes blinking all tweetybirdish being all "Mama knows what's best . . ." but this time she was like staring darla down the whole time and gritting her teeth. very strange. I think oprah noticed too because she goes, "wow that was big! big, big big! back in a minute."

For the first time in my life I didn't dive for the remote when a commercial came on. I just lay there, alone on a king-size bed (everything's bigger in Texas) and let the weight-loss pill ad wash over me while I thought about Darcy. what would she be like if she had a different mother? would she be more normal? would she still be a star? would she be more like me?

what if I had a different mother? would I have been less mean to her?

anyway after the commercial they came back in and they were talking about the transition from being the mother of a teen to being the mother of an adult or something. all I know is TWICE darcy said, "It's really really *liberational* to realize what feelings you have that are really yours and what feelings you have that you have been taught to have."

I was like "liberational"?

oprah goes so you're kind of looking at yourself and separating your nature from your nurture . . . finding out who you are independent of your family and mother" and darcy goes yeah I guess something like that and then she goes and I'm also starting to make my own choices, including choosing my own friends. now she was REALLY glaring at darla.

and something about the way she said it made me think she was talking about me. I don't know why. maybe it's because I've always known that if it was up to darcy I wouldn't have been fired. but darla got paranoid and did it for her and now she's got no one on the tour to hang out with anymore.

it made me want to see her. but at the same time it made me really nervous about seeing her.

I realized I was humming "be with me reality."

I had a quick IM with evan.

KellyKelSoCal321: want to come to new york next weekend?

SlipKnotRules933111: sure sounds fun

KellyKelSoCal321: that's it?

SlipKnotRules933111: what?

KellyKelSoCal321: see you next friday.

BACK AT THE RIHGA ROYAL, 4:17 PM
(when Pashmina found out that's where darcy was staying she made sure we did, too . . . so Pashmina could reserve a bigger room)
Outfit: official "Pashmina with Love" tour jacket, not because anyone's making me wear it, but because I want to.
Mood: Ask again later.

I'm doing my best to avoid watching too much TV . . . the last thing I need to see is a promo for this big show. It's like they're advertising my own personal Armageddon. Not that it's definitely going to be a disaster, but lord knows it could be.

still sort of in awe about Pashmina's unexpected kindness. I sorta stopped trying to mention it to her, but it kind of, well, humbled me.

made it through the whole day of blocking and rehearsals and sound checks and stuff without running into darcy. or darla. thank god. I think I saw her once, way back in the theater, while we were rehearsing, and it looked like she was giving me the LOOK but I'm not sure, maybe I could have imagined it.

BACKSTAGE AT THE GARDEN, 3 PM (did I mention we were taping this at the Garden?)

Outfit: still in my Pashmina with Love tour jacket
Hair: so far no one's touched it today. so far.
Mood: at breakfast, optimistic. now, kinda terrified.
Fortune: Begin at the beginning. And never end.

---

had the most amazing donut this morning for breakfast. ok I had two. Pashmina's bodyguard brought them to us from the Donut Pub on 14th St. they were incredible. Like not too greasy, but nice and gooey.

I stuck my head in the media room where there was a closed-circuit tv hooked up to—get this—a joint press conference darcy and Pashmina were giving together down at Planet Hollywood. I was like WHAT?!?! I guess it was a good publicity stunt, though. it coulda been a catfight.

but they totally hugged and told everyone they were really, really, truly good friends and everything. I snickered. they said were united in their love for Celine Dion, who the show is supposedly in honor of. I snickered again.

I started thinking how weird it was that I didn't even know they were doing this press conference. Back in the day, darcy would have made me go with her except for that one time at the Krispy Kreme. mmm donuts. anyway all these reporters were asking them questions: (Reporter: "Darcy what's next for you?" Darcy: "I'm going to take it to the next level!" Reporter: "Pashmina how did you come up with your new image?" "Omigosh we just decided to straighten my hair! Dang! Image is just so overrated you guys!")

Then some reporter asked what they'd be performing at the show. Pashmina (in full stage makeup, which, let's face it, can be scary at a press conference) said that she would be opening the show with "Girls Want It, Pt. 2."

Darcy started laughing.

Pashmina looked at her like, What?

darcy giggled a little, then said, that would be really cool! but seriously, tho, I'll be opening the show tomorrow night with "Last Laugh."

Pashmina looked at her like she was insane.

they both gave nervous giggles before Pashmina saved it, "guess we have to go backstage and diva out after all" and laughed it off. but it was clear there was a very serious problem afoot.

within moments cell phones around the room erupted. I slipped out.

we were on break so I took off to meet evan. his flight had landed about an hour before, and I'd asked the hotel to send a car service to pick him up. he felt so important. we didn't talk about home, we didn't talk about the show, we just ate grilled cheeses and talked about America's Most Wanted. it was great.

on our way back to the garden I wondered what had happened with darcy and Pashmina. it was totally one of those situations that I was so glad I was not actually a part of.

then I got back to the garden and found out I actually *was* a part of it.

GARDEN, 6:30 PM

Outfit: Pashmina prides herself on her creative input. today that means we all have to wear pastel competition ballroom dancing dresses with peekaboo valentines cut out of the butt. mine is green. Humiliating *and* impractical!!

Mood: ever notice how "mood" is actually "doom" spelled backward?

I had just changed into this hideous dress (see above) when Bernie the Big Bodyguard Dude grabs my shoulder and goes, Pashmina needs you onstage. I was like, did I miss a rehearsal and he just goes, come with me.

he walked me, fast, through the halls. I felt like I was going to the principal's office, only scarier.

he walked me through a door to the stage area. we wound our way through the scaffolding and past the stage manager's station. I could hear darcy's valley girl texas voice (it's gotten more texas I noticed) going, "Look, all I know is they promised me the opener. I wouldn't have agreed to do the show otherwise."

she sounded pretty serious. I'm like oh no, I don't want to be here right now . . .

I stopped, but Bernie nudged me along.

there was a long pause, then about 40 voices started chattering all at once.

we rounded the corner and entered, stage left. it was so dramatic. in the middle of the massive, black-lacquered stage, there was a table and two chairs. they looked like they were floating on a superdeep black pool of water. everything reflected perfectly off the shiny stage.

in the two chairs were Darcy and Pashmina, facing each other like they were the president of the united states and the premier of china at a summit. they had their backs straight and their claws OUT. I couldn't figure out which one of them was blonder.

both of them had full battle makeup and hair, already prepped for their shows, but both were in identical white robes. darcy's robe was too small and her boobs were all over the place but then, it wouldn't be darcy without some cleavage. Pashmina's robe was too big. she was swimming in it. like it was her dad's or boyfriend's or something.

darcy had nine dancers behind her (I noticed they hadn't bothered to replace me) and Pashmina had seven. there were all these men in black . . . males and females, some sopranos style and some traditional. eileen was there, pacing, mumbling. I saw rashid in the background, he winked at me.

everyone was talking at each other or making that sucking-on-your-teeth sound or frantically dialing their cell phones.

darla was just standing there about four paces behind darcy, mumbling silently, facing me but looking at the back of darcy's head . . . then she moved her glance up to Pashmina and I could see her mouthing "how dare she how dare she" then she glanced up, saw me, and glazed over with the most intense LOOK she's probably ever mustered up. suddenly I felt really cold, especially right around the peekaboo valentine cutout part of my costume.

Bernie nudged me toward the table to join the other dancers behind Pashmina.

just then Pashmina leaned forward, looked down at the table, and whispered something superquietly.

no one heard her so everyone was like shh! SHH! SHHHH! what did she say? and it got SILENT in there and everyone leaned in and she said it again, superquietly.

"I open or I don't sing."

a moment of silence, then the place erupted. Panic. eileen wang was pacing like a maniac, going a mile a minute "we can work this out . . . we can work this out . . . we can work this out . . . ok . . . nobody panic, nobody panic." several of the men in black started shouting into their cells. the soprano wannabes were just shaking their heads and feeling the insides of their jackets. darla let out this groan, really really deep, like, "aauuuuugh!" darcy just smiled.

this man in black leaned in and whispered something

into her ear. she goes, "really!" and he goes, yeah, and whispered something else and then she whispered back, "you're right." she goes, "thanks so much!" and looked up at me. like, directly into my eyes.

everyone followed her gaze, all eyes on me now.

you know what? goes Darcy to Pashmina but still looking at me, Fine. you can open with one condition. I want only one thing. I want Kimball. I want her off your tour and back on mine.

I'm gagging, but I'm silent. Inside, I'm like WHAT? but outside, I'm shrinking into myself, smaller and smaller.

everyone else in the room was like Kimball, Kimball? who's Kimball? why do I know that name? Kimball, Kimball . . . what is it? who is it?

Pashmina leans in again, everyone shuts up again.

that's it? that's all you want? just k.k.? that's *it*? Fine, whatever. she's yours. AFTER she does my opener.

I was thinking what do you mean "that's *it*?" what do you mean "whatever"? don't you want me to stay?

then I realized EVERYONE IN THE PLACE suddenly knew what "Kimball" meant and they were all looking at me again. I soooo wanted to disappear right then. my whole strategy for this show, to stay low and tight and outta sight, was toast.

then I heard darla NO! NO! darcy! under no circumstances! listen to me. this is your mama speaking! I won't hear of it! I won't have that girl in our company. she started walking toward darcy, all, I won't have it is that clear? are you listening to your mama?

darla was striding confidently, strong, stroking that freakin' bug-eyed dog of hers punkin the Pekinese. "no this will not happen. darcy I need to see you alone please. *NOW.*" she walked right up to darcy, reaching out like she was going to take darcy by the elbow and lead her out. "Stand up, darcy."

darcy stood up, but instead of locking arms with darla, she threw up her hand in front of darla like a roadblock, barking "forget it." but darcy never took her eyes off me. she was boring into me. it was cool she was ignoring her mother and controlling her mother and keeping focused on me all at the same time. but it was a little scary, too.

darla, LOOK-enhanced darla, darted her eyes from darcy to me and back again.

darcy goes, "K.K.?" I just stared back. still staring. staring back and forth not blinking. It was like when evan and I were in the backseat and dad would offer ten cents to whoever won a staring contest between us two just to keep us quiet but he always won because I was never really good at it. but this time I did ok, no blinks. I didn't answer her, I just stared. darcy goes, "then it's settled. I'll expect you in my dressing room *immediately* after Pashmina's opening number. immediately. lordy we'll need to completely redo your hair and makeup."

and I was kinda terrified and overwhelmed and I really didn't know what the hell was going on but something about the way darcy was talking to me was like, I just went "ok" and then she gave me this teeny little smile but I recognized it and all of a sudden I was psyched.

I looked over at darla and saw that the LOOK had started to . . . um how can I put it . . . . jiggle. fast. not like how it would jiggle if she were sobbing or giggling, more like somewhere in between having had too much caffeine and trying to chew gum really really fast so you chew the sugar out so you can blow bubbles faster than whoever you're racing. also she was stroking Punkin the Pekinese really fast. his buggy eyes kept squinting up with each stroke as she pulled his skin up over his eyes from underneath. it was kinda gross. anyway so darla was jiggling. and with each jiggle the LOOK started to come apart.

"NO!" she hissed. "Darcy! No!"

she was just jiggling away and pixilating out, and it felt like it started to happen in slow motion or something because I started having the feeling that I had been standing there watching the LOOK turn to something that normally holds suspended fruit. it was not as much like the wicked witch melting thing in the Wizard of Oz as it seems. which was too bad considering what a nice tie-in that would have been. it was more like a staticky VHS recording.

darla took two paces back, struggling now to maintain even just a little bit of the LOOK.

"darcy?" she seethed, eyes now shifting to the back of darcy's hair.

"guys?" commanded darcy, motioning for a couple of men in black to go stand next to darla. not to like escort her out or anything more like to support her if she tipped over. but also maybe to stand in between her and darcy, you know, just in case anyone started swinging.

oh god imagine that.

anyway she and Pashmina stood up at the same time, spun around, and led their troops offstage. I just stood there for a second, watching darcy walk out.

darla reached out and grabbed darcy's arm saying don't do this baby trust mama. darcy just brushed off darla's arm (knocking Punkin the Pekinese on the head while she was at it, I was happy to notice, sorry PETA) and kept walking.

Just then, I noticed rashid again. he gave me one of his winks, and suddenly everything made sense.

STILL AT THE GARDEN, AROUND 8:15 PM

Outfit: Back in an "It's Darcy!!" tour jacket. Darcy gave me a new one since I threw the last one away.
Hair: My hair needs a SERIOUS break. it's been the longest summer of its life.
Fortune: Fame is addictive.

---

after the Pashmina performance (in which she first sang "Girls Want It, Pt. 2" and then did a duet of "Over the Rainbow" with The Dixie Chicks, oh yeah and the lighting was really messed up and she kept having to chase the spotlight . . . I heard she was rude to the crew or something . . .) anyway after that I busted into Darcy's dressing room. she goes oh lordy you still have Pashmina makeup on. ew. shaundree, can you start on her like that or should she wash it off?

shaundree was like Oh. My. God. and handed me a towel. Go wash that off.

I was like hold up a second. Darcy. what's the deal? I mean I was psyched to see her and all but I needed to know what was going on. and why.

and she says, Please, you don't belong with Pashmina. Lordy please wash your face we don't have much time. here's a headband. look, I saw your performance just now. I even saw you at that Teen Queen of the Universe pageant or whatever that was. are you aware how you look in those outfits?

shaundree goes, There's a mild alpha hydroxy scrub there next to you . . . use that. everyone in the room was focused on my face right now . . . on getting Pashmina off it and Darcy back on it.

darcy kept on, I mean seriously K.K.! That show, those outfits, that music it's not you. that is not the real K.K.

I was like, Oh and you know who the real K.K. is? cause I don't! I mean c'mon, K.K. isn't even my name! this whole life is fake! and you can't just trade me like a football player it's not cool!! I'm a person what about what I want? hand me that towel.

and she handed me a towel and was like, What are you talking about REAL? what do you mean this whole life is fake? what, you're going to tell me that your summer hasn't been real? this summer that you know as well as I do changed your life? news flash, but your REALITY this summer was this: dancing, performing, living kinda large. and don't get me wrong but I think you pretty much enjoyed it, didn't you? I mean, I know it was different before and I know it'll be different again but it wasn't any realer then. and it never will be any realer later. this is what you're doing now, that makes it real. take off your bra. here's a robe. oh god your brows are like GONE! Lordy! what happened to your brows? I felt like a mannequin, and not in a good way. here I was shedding one pop star's image for another pop star's image and wondering where in all this chaos my own image was.

I was like, Look I'm always going for realness in my performances and realness in my life but I haven't seen anything REAL this whole summer! not on your tour, not on hers! everything is just a big illusion!

and she goes, You don't get it do you? look, maybe I never really graduated high school, but I happen to know that REAL isn't something you can *try to be.* it's not something you chase. realness is not something out there. it's right here. what's real is what's now, where you are and what you're doing, now, today, whether you're being yourself or not. you don't get to choose what's real and what isn't. it all is. are you just biding your time waiting for something REAL? waiting for your REAL life to start? lordy k.k. you need to wake up. your life is happening right here. right now.

I just stared into the mirror. For what seemed like a really long time. Right here, right now.

I was like wow going on oprah really can change you ha ha.

she goes ok you look ok. here k.k. here's an altoid.

I go what about Darla.

and Darcy goes, in this air traffic controller voice, "Darla has left the building!" I was like huh? and darcy goes, Yeah darla is seriously on my nerves. she and I had it out while you were doing that dopey "Girls Want It" song. I mean she's my mom and all but she's seriously crowding

259

my personal space these days. you know what I mean? I mean, doesn't every teenage girl like DREAM of getting away from their mother, and here, look, I CAN!

oh my lordy look how cute your hair looks shaundree you're a goddess! anyway whatever I love her sorry god she's my mother but I'm not 12 years old anymore. I built her that big huge house with the guitar-shaped pool in east texas, I told her she needs to hang out there more. look here's your outfit.

darcy held out a couple of hangers and got all fashion television for a second describing it like she was some designer backstage at their show or something. "Rainbow tube top and yellow lowrider bellbottoms with a front slit and rainbow piping. whattya think?"

I was just like, Um looks great. I'd never seen darcy talk like this before. she was making sense.

she kept going. Anyway darla wasn't happy and she called me ungrateful she probably thinks my brain has been taken over by alien Swedish record producers or something but you know what one thing I know about my mom is when she gets into a tizzy you just gotta let her rip until it runs out. then she'll put her spin on it or whatever and say it was her decision and find another tizzy. shoot we don't have time to do your nails do we? look mine are glittery. oh well. anyway she'll chill out when she gets down there. besides it's not like I won't keep her on the payroll. I figure she can look after the construction of my museum. can you believe she wanted to go on howard stern tonight while I was performing here?

I was like museum? *Museum?*

then I was like, Dude you called her darla instead of mama.

and she goes, Yeah it's the new us. it's more real don't you think.

I go, I'm just happy to never have to see that freakin' dog again. we both cracked up.

I was like I like the new us. then she looks in the mirror and starts flicking her bangs and goes, "do you think my hair looks better than gwyneth's?"

I just go, "dude you have something in your teeth" and she goes "no WAY has it been there this whole time I hate you!"

I handed her some floss and I was like c'mon let's go. we walked over toward the stage.

where are the other dancers? what song are we doing anyway? I asked. she goes, just you and me k.k. we're doing "be with me, reality."

I panicked. What? We've never rehearsed it! she goes I'm melody, you're harmony, just sing. you really can, you know. besides, too late. we go on in one min.

I started breathing heavy.

we walked past gwen stefani, beyonce, and gloria estefan on the way to the stage, but I barely even noticed.

GARDEN, 10:15 PM

I didn't have time to think about it. I just sang.

I thought getting THERE when I was dancing was something, but getting THERE when you're singing is way more intense. Like, way more. it was big. scary and big.

in fact I was really proud of myself. As soon as we started to sing it, the song didn't seem nearly as cheesy as when we first wrote it, for some reason. maybe because when we wrote it, I was being cynical. this time I just gave in and sang it and I felt it.

"Be with me, reality!"

it was much catchier, much prettier than I'd remembered it being. I got into it.

most of the audience was actually quiet for it—and they got quieter as we continued singing. (that NEVER happens at those Divas Alive shows! usually everyone in the audience is like chatting the whole time.) I blew a couple of notes but I played it pretty safe and it worked. I just concentrated on my harmonies, I let darcy take the lead, and we came together and it worked pretty well.

I knew even evan probably got into it. that is, if he made the show on time.

262

I imagined dad was listening too, hopefully proud of me for harmonizing on the spot.

darcy was happy, I could tell. I decided I really did like her, even if I didn't understand the first thing about her and even if I could never handle the insanity of being her "best friend" again. she's as brave as they come.

anyway, we sang it. we didn't get a standing ovation or anything . . . I mean, most of the people at those shows are like record execs and their assistants . . . but the applause we *did* get was for US, not just darcy. it felt real.

Real.

FRIDAY AUGUST 30

RIHGA, 11:59 PM

Outfit: Darcy's own personal tour jacket. she left it on her chair when she left. like she needs it. I figure she can spare it and I don't know, I could use the souvenir. I wonder if there's money in it ha ha. maybe I could eBay it. ha ha just KIDDING! I would never. *Ever.* (wink)

Hair: I am so tempted to shave it all off right now. it's like straw, I'm not kidding. they have tortured it this summer. I need tito bad. this could be his biggest job ever. he'll like mash a mango in it and infuse Egyptian nile river oil with French lavender or something and make me wear a do-rag for like a weekend or something and it'll look amazing again.

Mood: tired. that kind of tired where you blink really slow and the air feels cooler in your lungs than usual.

I skipped the afterparty to wait for evan to show up backstage after the show. but true to form, he was nowhere to be seen. darcy ran off to meet jesse going, "how long are you in town? just tonight? well page me let's get together when I'm in cali, ok?" I was like, um, ok. is that it? I guess for her it doesn't feel like anything's over.

I wonder if she's right.

finally at like 11:30 the security people were like you have to leave now and I was like damn where's my bro. I kept checking for a page from him but none came. I

264

decided to just go back to the hotel because I knew he knew where the rihga was . . . when he asked where I was staying earlier he was like no WAY that's where Mike Tyson stays I was like really and he goes I think so and he goes I was reading about it online the other day. it's on 54th St. he is so misunderstood you know. I was like whatever anyway the point is he knows where the riga is.

at least I was hoping he does.

so I did my now routine taxicab hail and went back up to the rihga. there, in the lobby, was evan. with tito! tito came racing over to me and goes, "you KILLED it!" and I was like, shut up! omiGOD! what are you doing here and he goes, you KILLED it! and he wrapped his arms and legs around me like a little kid. I was just like, omigod how MUCH do I LOVE you? when did you GET here? and he goes, girl! what's up with this hair. we need a Cosmetics Plus, quick!

I looked over his shoulder and there was mom. no way! tito and evan must have convinced her to come.

she came up and gave me a hug and goes, "I saw the show tonight. I made sure I was on time. You were beautiful." she didn't sob Lifetime Television style, but she had tears dripping off the end of her nose.

I wiped her nose with the sleeve of darcy's jacket. Thanks mom. I smiled. can we go home now?

she goes yeah, we got a lot to do.

TUCKER SHAW lives in New York City, where he crosses paths with celebrities every time he walks out the door. He also watches what some people think is "too much" TV. But Tucker has still managed to write several award-winning books, including the critically praised love story *Flavor of the Week*.